Pink Boots in Black Puddles

LILA WHITE

Dedication

To my two daughters.
My puddle jumpers.

Disclaimer

This book is a memoir. It reflects the author's present recollections of experiences over time. Names, characteristics, and locations have been changed. Some events have been compressed and some dialogue has been recreated. Memory has its own story to tell, but the author has done their best to tell a truthful story. This story is about their emotional truth and does not reflect others' ideas or feelings.

prologue

LIFE WAS SUPPOSED to be the happily-ever-after I had always dreamed about. The marrying young and having a bucket load of children. Happy and successful in life. I thought I'd found the perfect man to become my husband and I was well on my way to my dream life. Explain to me how it goes from perfect to a puddle of blackness? How did he end up with an exotic dancer in a foreign country while I was left with the children and the mess that was left behind? This was not part of the plan - the plans "to prosper me, to give me a hope and a future".

Fast forward several years, and after many twists and turns I learn to move forward, and grab hold of the adventure of my life. I experience so much with family, friendships, travel, horses and an incredible amount of fun along the way. And after what seems like forever, I recover from the first puddle, pull on my new pink boots and try the whole happily-ever-after dream again.

I am so prepared this time around! I have learnt from past mistakes, I have taken back ground, and I am in a perfect place of readiness. This would be the real happily-ever-after, so I thought... instead, I found a bigger black puddle trying to swallow me up. Once again, someone I love quit on me. I am still splashing through this puddle as I write, but there will be an end to this season too, and I will move through it and beyond it. After this, I am sure a new pair of pink boots will be in order!

Despite the pain it can bring, I believe life is just one huge adventure. It is to be lived to the full, and I will not live an on-the-sidelines kind of life. I will finish this race knowing I have run it well, with my whole heart. Within these pages, I hope you will find encouragement and hope for your own circumstances and enjoy the journey with me. The journey of a story that is totally true — except for the parts I made up.

Chapter 1

CHILDHOOD

I T WAS FOUR days before my third birthday when I arrived with my family on the shores of Sydney, Australia.

My parents had made the decision to leave England and move to where my grandparents now lived, in a popular beaches' region. We travelled by Ellinis, a Greek ship, as "10-pound Pommies". We were very blessed as we had a cabin with a porthole. A lot of other "10 pound" families were not so lucky, as family members were often separated onto different ships and travelled in an inside cabin.

I was a toddler, which of course means I don't have clear memories of this time – but what I do have is a collection of anecdotes handed down via family legend.

If there's one story that exemplifies our British unpreparedness for the Australian climes and culture, it's the one about Bondi Beach. My dad, being of the English persuasion, couldn't swim – so one would think a trip to the beach could wait until he'd had a lesson or two. But the heat of a sweltering Aussie summer was a far more pressing issue, it seems. February in Sydney is not so easy to deal with when you've just come from the British Isles in the dead of winter. Dad concluded that the only thing to be done was to go to the beach - and obviously that beach should be the famous Bondi. That's right folks, he had no idea how to swim, nor what to do when a wave hits, but that was not about to stop him.

Now you are probably jumping a few sentences ahead in your mind, assuming I'm going to tell you he gets caught in a rip - but not a chance; this is my story and therefore it never goes down the obvious route! What happened next was far more colourful. Picture it, if you will: my dad is peacefully enjoying the clear summer sky and cool water of the Pacific, when he suddenly spies some grey fins emerging from the water. He's watched *Jaws*. Surely this can only mean one thing. He starts screaming, "Sharks! Get out of the water!" Crowds of people panic and frantically stumble out of the water left, right and center; Dad is terrified and no doubt close to a heart attack. However, upon further observation by more astute beachgoers, it turns out it was just a pod of dolphins. Welcome to Australia, Dad!

Our little family of four, consisting of my parents and my brother Anton, who was two years older than me, settled into sharing a home with my mum's parents. This wasn't ideal, as my grandfather had a way of manipulating my mum into obedience. He had never treated her well, and very much dominated all those around him. He belittled my father and turned my mum into the housemaid. Mum now had to keep the house clean and make all the family meals, while my dad was expected to find a job as quickly as possible and financially provide for everyone – including the grandparents! My parents suffered through this for a season until they finally got out from under my grandfather's tyranny and moved to an apartment close by. Finally, we were a family of four, in our own little space.

Isn't it interesting how people mistreat us, and we justify their behaviour? With my grandad the excuse was always, "It's hard for him because of the war." But guess what, people: he was like this before the war! He had never treated my mum with love or respect. As she was the only daughter of three children, and the eldest, it was considered her job to keep house and look after the family. At this point you may be thinking, "What about my grandmother?" Well, Grandma is a bit of an anomaly. Supposedly she was fragile and not capable of looking after the family. But it seems she was robust enough to go and work as a secretary, something she clearly enjoyed much more than housekeeping. I wonder if one of her goals in working was to escape her husband each day?

I remember mum telling me that if my grandad's dinner was cold when placed in front of him, he would throw it at the wall. There was a lot going on in that home that never gets spoken about; if you talked to my uncles, they would tell you all was well in the home.

Let's go back to our apartment: it was small, but it was home. Dad secured a job in a local supermarket, and mum became a Tip Top bread courier. I have two standout memories from this time. One is of the times mum would take me with her to work but would leave me in the back of the Tip Top van while she dropped off loaves of bread to shops. I had to sit in the dark waiting and would end up smelling of bread; I am amazed I'm not afraid of dark, small spaces.

My second memory is of the times she didn't take me to work, and I was left with the neighbour instead. This memory makes me feel uneasy. I remember this neighbour watching hours of television, something similar to *Judge Judy*, and I had to sit still, not make a sound and wait for her to acknowledge me. She had a son who was the same age as me, about four years old, and she would put us both in her double bed for a nap. The problem was, her son wet the bed on several occasions, and I was blamed for this transgression. We would both wake up wet, because I would be sleeping next to him, and as she didn't want to embarrass her son the blame was placed squarely on me. Give me a bread van any day rather than this neighbour!

When I was five, my youngest brother was born, and we moved from the apartment to a bigger house. Now there is a story to tell, right here. It is a bit on the weird side, but then, nothing much about my story is normal. The house was haunted. Yes, that's what I'm telling you. I was young, so although I knew things went on, I can't remember the full details. My oldest brother remembers more. There would be hands hovering in doorways, and lights turning on and off. Household items such as drinking glasses would get moved around. My brother's favourite teddy, called Foxy, was once found high up in a palm tree. In those days the banks used to give you plastic money boxes, and I remember Mum cutting our money box to shreds, because it had flown across the room at her. A lot of unexplained things happened in that house and consequently we moved out.

So, what's my take on these strange happenings? I would have to say I'm not a believer in ghosts. At least, not in the traditional sense: spirits of the departed sticking around to bother the relatives, and all that. I do, however, believe in the supernatural. There is an entire realm that exists and operates, outside of this natural realm that we can see, hear and touch. I can't tell you why this happened to my family, but I can tell you that my mum was very open to this type of thing, and her brother (my uncle) opened himself up to this spirit realm, too, through transcendental meditation and other New Age practices.

From these observations as a child, I concluded that my mum and my uncle's dabbling in the occult and the New Age was messing with my family - which tells me it was not of God, and therefore was to be avoided. My uncle organised a seance to find out who the ghost was. His conclusions were that this was a female ghost we were dealing with, apparently hailing from my mum's past life in the French Revolution. Supposedly she died saving my mum's life. My dad on the other hand, told me that he was the one moving the glasses around, because he did not believe in all this poppycock. I'll leave you to draw your own conclusions!

I think now is the perfect time to make this book a little bit more interesting, by introducing a couple of characters that are going to feature heavily. I have named them, Sinister and Victory. These two will be prominent throughout and will lead us on this little journey through my life. Sinister makes many appearances, namely wherever those 'black puddles' of my life appear - while Victory is most prominent when I pull on those metaphorical 'pink boots' and dance on through.

At this juncture, allow me to explain the title I've chosen for my book. I have always loved pink. It makes me happy. I loved it as a little girl, and never saw the need to 'outgrow' it. To this day, pink features heavily in my home, my wardrobe, and my office. It's the colour of my car, and, yes, it's the colour of several pairs of my shoes – including boots. In fact, I've lost count of how many pairs of pink boots I've owned over the years. (I even got married in pink boots, once—but that's a story for later.) As for the 'black puddles' part of my title; as you will have gathered by now, this represents the unpleasant curve-balls life has thrown my way. I've lost count of those, too! Nevertheless, you'll see how my pink boots have always seen me through the worst of the black puddles... and, as you can tell, I'm still here to tell my story!

For now, back to my childhood.

One day when I was very young, I came home from school and taught my brother a swear word. I had no idea what a swear word was, but we went marching around the house chanting, "piss off!" (Scandalous, I know). My dad came home and heard us chanting our hearts out. He jumped to the conclusion that my brother, being older than me, must have taught me this word, and immediately marched him to the bathroom where he washed his mouth out with soap. I don't even think I felt bad about it at the time; I was that young that I didn't fully understand what had happened. My brother, though, has never forgotten that he had to eat soap because of me. Poor Anton!

In my primary years, I was a bit of a loner on the school front. I played the cornet in the school band; we settled in a semi-rural suburb and my parents owned the local supermarket. We moved from house to house within our community, often just carrying our furniture from one house to the next. Quite literally, my dad and my brothers would carry the beds down the street, around the corner to the next house that we were moving into. It was quite embarrassing. Mum loved creating new spaces; she was in her happy place when she could create a comfortable home. People always commented on her flair for making a home inviting. It must be in the DNA as I've followed in her footsteps; in my adult years I've always loved to decorate and make a place homely and welcoming.

I was allowed a great deal of freedom growing up. I did whatever activities were on offer: ballet, Girl Scouts, and riding horses. My love for horses remains, and as an adult I could not have survived some of my darkest days without them. My mum was very involved in all my extra-curricular activities, but Dad, not so much. Having played in a brass band in England, he did encourage me with my music - but he didn't come to many of my performances. Like most dads, he was busy working. I don't remember him coming to see me perform in ballet, or watching me ride my horse, or attending a school function - but he was very involved with my brothers' lives. He coached their soccer teams, and the three of them would watch unlimited amounts of sports on television. To me my dad was either working, with the boys, or watching football. Here is probably where 'Sinister' started to play a part in my life. I would try so hard to be part of the boys' club, by going to the speedway on a Saturday night - even though it was forever away, and I got car sick - or assisting in coaching the under 5's soccer. But Sinister still made me feel like I was never good enough for my dad to spend time with. I think my parents had a very old-school mindset, where the father had the boys and the mother looked after all thing's 'girl'. But try telling that to a young girl in pink boots, who just wanted time with her dad. Sinister was laying his trap.

My younger brother, Jayden, was a handful to say the least. He would be the first to agree. If he'd grown up now, he would probably have been diagnosed with ADHD - and that was likely a result of owning a supermarket with an unlimited supply of sugar. He was hyperactive and scary. My older brother, Anton didn't help Jayden's behaviour, and knew exactly what to do to antagonise him, mercilessly teasing him until he broke. However, because Anton was seven years older and much bigger than Jayden, revenge was not an option. So instead, I was the one to be terrorised by our whirlwind little brother. Terrorised is no overstatement; Jayden would chase me around the house with an axe - I kid you not - and I remember an incident where I grabbed a lounge cushion just as the axe came down upon me. Definitely a moment where 'Victory' was present and made sure I was kept safe!

I hear you asking, where are the adults while this is going on? At the supermarket, of course, working. I am sure my brothers were no different to other boys, but they were often left unsupervised, and this resulted in mischief and mayhem. They would put the two cats under the blanket together just to watch them fight or climb up onto the roof and throw chickens off, to see how far they could fly. They were, and still are, highly competitive and constantly egged each other on. I tried to fly under the radar and keep to myself, but how is that possible with siblings? They would often use me to referee their battles.

We didn't have a lot of money, but my mum was very creative. We lived in a half-built house for a while; the back door opened onto open space as the verandah had never been added. It only had one bedroom, so Mum made a fancy partition out of fabric, and my brothers shared half the room with my parents. Meanwhile, my room was an unfinished hallway which couldn't even fit a bed, and yet again my mum came up with an innovative idea: she built my bed on top of the wardrobe. I loved it. It was such a novelty. Nobody else had a bed on top of a wardrobe. I had my bed up there for about a year. The bathroom was outside and was home to funnel web spiders, and the toilet was an old dunny, which is a tin can that my poor father had to empty every week.

I am sure my parents found this a very challenging place to live, but it was all they could afford and as for us kids we loved it. It was on acres and backed onto National Park, so we were always outside. I remember our pet goat, a white one, named Billy (very original), who like many goats was pushy, and head-butted us at times. My mum accidentally ran over him once, and he had to have a cast on his leg - but even this didn't stop him from butting you over.

At Christmas time there wasn't a lot of money for presents, but Mum always came up with wonderful gifts that she could create with her own hands. There was one Christmas when she was inspired by *The Sound of Music*, and she built us this incredible puppet stage and all these puppets to go with it, based on the characters from the famous movie. The puppets were made from fabric – Mum was a great sewer and artist. There was an elaborate stage, carved, and painted bright colours. I was the winner of every book parade at school because of the amazing costumes Mum made. One year I went as a giant jam sandwich made from boxes from the shop, with the bread and the jam oozing out of it, all painted on. The next year I was 'The Lonely House' painted on a box. It was truly remarkable. It really does show that a happy childhood is not always about owning everything and having all the modern conveniences - it's about making the most of what you have. I think we were one of the last families amongst my friends to get a colour television.

For vacations, we went to my uncle's farm in Bellingen. We had a Mazda Bongo, a van that was popular in the 1970s. It didn't have back seats, so mum made a platform to go on the floor with pillows, so that me and my brothers could sleep the eight hours it would take to get to the farm. Being a sufferer of travel sickness though, for me the trip was always pretty rough; much of it was spent with my head in a bucket.

Our holidays in Bellingen were memorable for all kinds of reasons, not always good ones. Trips to Bellingen were another of those times when Sinister was prowling my life. To give you some context to our Bellingen trips, you have to remember that this was the '70s: an era of hippies, flower power, wholefoods, and living off the land—and the northern NSW town of Bellingen was an epicentre for this way of life.

One memory that stands out from these holidays, is having to eat pumpkin pie made with wholemeal flour, probably made by my mum and my aunty; it was so dry I struggled to swallow it. I laugh now about how food can create such powerful memories. My brother Anton was traumatised as a very little boy while still living in England, when our aunty made him eat his peas – by force. To this day, he cannot stomach peas. Then there is the much more pleasant memory of Mum making what we termed "pommies", which consisted of broken up pieces of bread in warm milk. She would make it for us when we felt sick; it sounds disgusting now to be honest, but when we were kids, we loved it.

But getting back to Bellingen. Being the hotbed of 'getting back to nature' that it was, nudity featured highly in this town. Keep in mind that I was between the ages of 8 and 12 when we were taking our regular trips to hippy-ville, and this place was full of naked adults. No one thought clothes were necessary except us children. Yes, that is correct, even my parents stripped off when they got to the valley.

Now I know this may not seem such a big deal to some, but unfortunately for me there was a gentleman whose behaviour around me was bordering on inappropriate. He never actually touched me - but would spend large amounts of time sitting and chatting with me when no other adults were around, and yes, he was naked. You know what I'm talking about, that unmistakable feeling that something just isn't right; but how do you explain that to an adult and not look like an over-reacting child? I couldn't tell them at the time. Needless to say, I was very grateful when my parents grew out of their hippy phase, and our trips to the valley came to an end.

Don't get me wrong, my childhood wasn't a disaster; I knew my parents loved me and they never denied us anything. They were just very busy trying to run a business and, like every other family, pay the bills, bring up three children, and allow them to experience all that life had to offer.

Chapter 2

TEEN YEARS

I T IS TIME, my dear readers, to step into the wonderful teen years. Let's be honest, for many of us, there is nothing wonderful about being a teenager. Sinister becomes your closest companion and you are facing down all sorts of unpleasantness. At least, that was my experience.

Let's set the scene: I'm just about to turn thirteen and I am ugly; I know this because that is what my brother tells me. I have braces, I'm really skinny, with an extra large nose and frizzy hair. It just wasn't your average pretty-girl-next-door look. How hard is it to fit into that stereotypical teen image, when you simply aren't blessed with the goods? Sinister managed to use my brother's taunting to drive home the point of my inability to be even mildly appealing. It was not an easy time.

I was very involved with horses, though, (Victory was at work here), and I have no doubt that this kept me from falling into the abyss of total despair. Nevertheless, the hormones want what the hormones want, and they wanted to be loved by a boy.

Before plunging into the rabbit hole of boys, let me tell you a bit more about my love of horses. I spent a huge proportion of my time at a horse-riding school, where I would ride their horses, help muck out the stables and just hang out. The girl who was in charge of the school was four years older than me, and I idolised her. Throughout my teens we became the best of friends; that is, until I started dating a guy she liked—but more about that later.

When I reached the age of 11, I begged my parents for a horse, and I found one being advertised on the noticeboard at the local shops, for one hundred dollars. My parents, being as they are, couldn't say no; after all this was my passion. His name was Rusty, and I threw myself with gusto into the all-consuming role of owning and caring for a horse. He lived at my friend's property. Unfortunately, though, six months after I bought him, I broke my arm while jumping on a friend's trampoline, and I was unable to ride Rusty for the next four months. My brave mother decided the only thing to do was to ride him herself, but she had no experience, and horses know when that is the case. Rusty bucked my mum to the ground so many times, that it wasn't long before Rusty was unrideable. It was decided that he had to go back to his original family until I could ride again. Tragedy struck one night, when there was a break in on the property and Rusty freaked out. He jumped the fence, and in his fright fell off a cliff. He was found dead at the bottom with a broken neck. It was heartache for me, but I've no doubt it was a relief for my parents, as my mum had become terrified of him, and they were paying for his board while I wasn't riding.

About a year later, with me being still mad on horses, my parents purchased a stock horse, Little Boy Blue. He was magnificent: blue grey in colour with strawberry roan (speckle) on his rump. We would ride off together, cantering around the local bush trails and loving life. This pre-teen girl couldn't have been happier. But alas, another disaster was about to strike. Little Boy Blue came down with colic which means severe gastro pain. It is a dangerous condition for horses as they tend to roll on the ground to try and rid themselves of the pain, but in doing so, it twists their intestines. My mum stayed up an entire night, walking him around so that he wouldn't lie down. In the morning, she rang the vet, and his prognosis was, "This horse is fine, no need to worry". Mum came home exhausted but relieved, and I was ecstatic that my pony was going to be ok. Tragically though, you guessed it, readers, when mum and I went to check on him a couple of hours later he was dead. The grief I felt over this was overwhelming, and to this day I still struggle with how I feel about the vet that misdiagnosed him. I vowed to never get another horse—and so, what was next? Boy obsession.

Sinister was very prevalent in my twelfth year of living. I had lost my beautiful horse, and even though I still went to the riding school every week, it wasn't the same. There were some very dark days, and I would often spend hours sitting next to funnel web spider holes, daring myself to stick my finger in. "No-one would ever know it was deliberate," I thought, "I would just die from a spider bite: tragic, but in no way suspicious." I listened endlessly to sad songs, and I decided I would become a nun, inspired by *The Sound of Music*. During this particularly dark season of my life, I remember a long-lost cousin coming to visit, and he snuck into my room one night and, while I was asleep, kissed me. And it wasn't just a peck. I woke up to an unwanted tongue down my throat from a largely unknown relative who was two years older than me. He then went and bragged to my older brother, who teased me without mercy. I was horrified that this had happened, and so embarrassed. To them, I was just a plaything to be taunted and trampled on. I felt like my life was just an amusing sport for people to use and abuse for their entertainment. I was insecure, lonely, and felt very ugly. My brothers teased me relentlessly and my friends had started to turn nasty.

My beautiful mum could obviously see I was struggling, but she didn't have the skills to dig deep and really talk to me. Instead, she came upon a program called Aunty and Uncles – in which a troubled teen from the city, would come stay at a home in the suburbs like ours. The city kid gets to experience life a little differently, and we get the experience of hosting and building a new friendship. That's how Ruby entered my life. A year older than me, and street wise, Ruby's mother was an alcoholic and her sister a prostitute. Needless to say, she came with all sorts of issues—but I admired her. We became the best of friends, and she most definitely pulled me out of my place of despair, by distracting me fully.

Ruby would come to stay every second weekend, and she talked non-stop boys. She was a breath of fresh air for a lonely suburban girl like me—but was she 'Team Victory' or 'Team Sinister'? Given that my parents gave us kids way too much freedom, we were able to run amok. Ruby was older, actually had boobs - and big ones, unlike skinny flat chested me - and she smoked; so cool. Although my new bestie smoked, I'm grateful now that I never took up the habit and never even tried one. I would, however, hold her ciggie, so I would look as cool as her.

So, I'm now thirteen, I have a new and confident friend, and a brother two years older than me. What comes next? Yes, you guessed it - we enter the era of inappropriate teen behaviour. Sinister was very much around at this time, egging us teenagers on in our questionable decisions - but looking back I now see that Victory was also a very consistent presence, keeping me from making many bad choices. Let us now step into the world of teenage angst.

Anton, now 15, was becoming very interested in my friends and had his eye on one girl, Di, who he hoped to date. Meanwhile Ruby had developed a crush on one of Anton's mates. Who was the common denominator? Me. There was only one thing to be done; let's set up me, to date one of Anton's friends. That way, everyone will be happy. We will be a triple threat. I really think my parents should've locked us up at this stage, but they were oblivious to all the shenanigans. Our plan worked. Tom started dating me; my brother dated my friend Di, and Ruby was with Drew. We had a lot of fun, going for swims at the local waterfall, playing football (mostly so the boys could watch Ruby's chest bounce), hanging out, and, of course, making out.

One weekend we built a two-storey cubby at the back of our garage, and this became our 'place'. We would spend hours in there, and let's just say it wasn't to discuss our schoolwork. Spin the bottle was definitely a game of choice, along with many other games of mischief. I'm ashamed to admit it, but I once went home from that cubby with my neck covered in love bites. I cringe now thinking about it. I was grounded for two weeks, but how can parents enforce such punishment when they aren't around to see it through? They can't. At this point I should clarify that while my parents were always at the shop working, the shop was literally only two doors down – so they were never that far away. But that didn't keep us teens from trouble.

There was this food game we often played, where you would blindfold someone and get them to try a food (imagine doing that today with all the different food allergies kids suffer!). One time my brother decided to make it a drink dare, and his friend downed a large glass of mixed spirits. It didn't end well. He was so intoxicated. We were trying to sober him up under the shower at our place (I know, so effective), when his parents came to pick him up. I, of course had nothing to do with it - but Anton was busted big time.

It was also at this age that I told my biggest lie. It was very elaborate, but it had to be convincing. I told my parents that as part of a school project, I had to camp out at the bottom of our garden and learn survival skills. They believed me - and allowed myself and a couple of friends to set up camp. What was actually at play was that our boyfriends were going to hang out at a cubby house close by, and after midnight, they would sneak on over. I felt terrible about lying, but a girl had to do what a girl had to do. We girls were giggly and excited as expected, and we could not wait for midnight. Our sneaky plan never came to fruition though; I think we all fell asleep. Once again, Victory saw to it that my innocence stayed intact.

All good times must come to an end, and after only a short six months, Tom broke up with me. He told me it was because Anton was always pressuring him into doing favours; because after all, he had leverage – he was the one that got us two together. Whatever the reason for the breakup, my world came crashing down. Ruby and Drew also drifted apart, and after a year of friendship, Ruby stopped visiting. As for Anton, he would go on to date a few of my friends; I was his source. In years to come, that would all change and I would become my younger brother Jayden's source.

Bereft after my breakup, I plunged back into the horse life, and hanging out with my friend, June – the girl in charge of the horse-riding school. She was super cool, I looked up to her – while I was 14, she was 18 and driving. Now, a few years' age gap between friends is nothing when you're an adult – but when you're still a kid, under the legal age, and your friends are all adults, it gets iffy. June introduced me to her new crowd: a bunch of 21-year-old guys. I was a flirt and at the time didn't even consider my age; in my mind it was simple, these were my friends, and they were boys. (But in fact, they weren't, - they were men). I started dating Clifton. He was 21. I was 14. What on earth was I thinking? I was a child, and I was star-struck by an older man. I'm not saying he was bad. It's just that he was an adult. You'd be right to ask, "What on earth was *he* thinking?" - except that we all know what he was thinking. We dated for three months, until I realised what a mistake I had made: he was after something I wasn't prepared to give. This is where Victory steps in and opens my eyes. The lights went on, and I suddenly saw where this was headed.

I had ample opportunities to lose my virginity to any of these boyfriends, but I still had that whole nun-thing buzzing in my head, and the fear of falling pregnant, and disappointing my parents, far outweighed my desire. Besides that, I was still young, even though my friends were so much older. I was naive. Sure, I came across as fun, confident, and beyond my years, dressing in bright, bold colours, giving off the impression I was savvy - however I was anything but. I broke it off with Clifton, and there was such relief when that happened.

Where were my parents during these three months? Why on earth would they allow me to date a man? Good questions, and I did ask my mum years later. Her response was, "I didn't think you would listen. You are sensible enough to make your own decisions and we all have our own mistakes to make." Dad was too busy trying to control Anton and left mum to deal with me. Mum was no doubt right, I would have dated him with or without her permission - but it would have spoken volumes to me if I had known she didn't approve. This relationship could have ended very badly, and my mum would have been filled with regret. That is why I thank God that Victory always had my back.

Not long after this debacle, I was given another pony, Zapp. He was a great companion for me to enjoy. I would tuck my school uniform into my jeans, throw on his bridle, and we would then go down to the local oval and race around it without a saddle. Being such a horsey town, there were of course jumps set up on the oval for the local horse riders, and I remember one afternoon I decided to attempt some jumps without a saddle. This didn't end well; I ended up in hospital with concussion. I never told my mum that I sort of 'forgot' to put a saddle on! Oh, to be young and reckless. Anyway, when you own a horse, falling off is pretty much part of the deal.

Three months after the Clifton breakup, my friend and I decided to catch the overnight train to Melbourne and visit some relatives of hers. Again: "Parents, I was fourteen! What were you thinking!" Of course, we met some guys on the train; they were in the army. Sinister is in control at this point. Army Mark flirted his way into my good graces and led me off to the toilet. How classy is that? After a time of kissing, he decided he wanted more. Victory to the rescue; I unlocked the door and high-tailed it out of there. The other very unfortunate incident on that ill-fated train trip was that a passenger fell off, into the path of an oncoming train. It was shocking and tragic, and we spent hours stationary while it all got sorted. It definitely put a dampener on the beginning of our adventure. Once we finally arrived in Melbourne and caught up on some sleep, though, we did have a fabulous time, shopping and eating and laughing and, of course, fantasising about the boys on the train.

I must add at this point, that my school was a little on the rough side; not the nicest environment for growing up through your difficult teen years. There was no lining up nicely to get on the bus. Instead, it was a daily game of what we termed 'rumble', everyone pushing and shoving their way on board in a bid to get the back seats. At the back of the bus, everyone smoked, so I was happy to get on last and stand up the front. Students in my school would regularly bring alcohol, get drunk and pass out in the bathrooms, and students would be so disrespectful of teachers. There was an incident when a poor student teacher came to the school and our class would hurl abuse at her all lesson, every lesson. Her class was just after food technology so whatever food was prepared during that class, became missiles to throw at her. It was distressing to watch, and the incident made it onto the TV news. I used to get picked on myself so I knew what the bullying was like, and my heart would break for her. I must add the fact that this student teacher was transgender - no easy feat in the 80s. She was a uni student in her 20s who went from Robin to Roberta, a big woman with big hands, and the kids mercilessly poured out their hatred.

Liquid paper and glue sniffing was all the rage, too. I enjoy learning, but there was no way I was going to learn much at this school. It was definitely another one of those seasons where Victory was looking out for me.

During this time of life, my older brother Anton and I started to drift apart. I actually think he dated someone who wasn't one of my friends for once. He started hanging out with guys who misbehaved, stealing cars for joyrides, smoking dope and just being generally unsavoury. I remember he was always in trouble. In his place, my younger brother Jayden and I started to bond, and he would often come with me to see Zapp and have a ride. Jayden was a very clever kid. I remember he would set up a cardboard shop outside the supermarket, selling all his old comics and matchbox cars, and making quite a bit of money from it. From a young age, he knew how to get what he wanted. If only I could have known how his skills of persuasion would be used on girls; and just how many of my girlfriends, he would sleep with; and just how many hearts he would break - I might have decided to keep him at a distance.

As you can see, it was a typical teenage life that most of the time I loved. Lots of time outside, with no such thing as computer games to distract us. Maybe if there was, we would have behaved better. I do believe having horses during these years was a saving grace; it kept me busy, and with the help of Victory, I remained relatively unscathed. I turned 15 and a new chapter began.

Chapter 3

FIFTEEN & DATING RALPH

VICTORY TAKES CENTRE stage in the beginning of this chapter of my life, as this is where God and his son Jesus make an entrance into my life. I was always very aware that there was a God (probably from that *Sound of Music* obsession), but I didn't know what to do with this knowledge. My dad went to church every Sunday night, at the local Uniting Church, but we never joined him; we had important television to watch. Back in England, Dad was in the Methodist church, where he was the youth leader for a while, and there was a time when he wanted to be a pastor. His parents were Methodist and passed on the tradition to him. God was always in our family. Like many families, we all went to a church service at Christmas and Easter. But

Dad never pushed his faith on us. To be honest I think church was a bit of 'me' time for him. Mum, meanwhile, was wrapped up in New Age stuff, influenced by her brother, who was into things like reading auras, and transcendental meditation. (As you may have guessed this is the same uncle who lived at Bellingen). Our house was very mixed up spiritually! My mum also had another brother who was, and still is, a strong Christian. He and his wife have been a big support to me over the years. They've often seen more in me than I have myself. They've always prayed for me and encouraged me for which I'm deeply grateful.

My first real encounter with the things of faith was when June and I went along to an outreach café at the local shops, and from there we were invited to a little church within riding distance. So, we decided to ride our horses to church the following Sunday. I loved it. The salvation message was finally explained to me in a way that made sense, and I committed my heart to Jesus. I was now one of those "born-again believers". I fitted straight into the Christian lifestyle and loved church. I felt like I'd come home. It all made sense to me – the friendship, the sense of community, and the spiritual connection I found there. All my life I'd had an idea of who God was, and as a child I would look out the window at night and find the brightest star and pray. Then, when I found faith, I realised I had been praying to God my whole life. The pastor at this church was lovely and he and his wife made me feel very welcome. I would hang out at their house often and stay for dinner. I never felt uncomfortable around them.

Six months after my conversion, into the church walks Ralph. Tall, tanned and muscly, with wavy, sun-kissed beach-hair and bright blue eyes, he was there as a Bible college student, on a three-week practical placement. He was 20, he was Godly, and boy was he good looking. Clearly this guy must be for me. But of course, that is also what all the other single girls thought, and I was the youngest, at only 15. He was definitely the centre of attention. June was besotted too, so as the younger, I did the admirable thing and backed off. During his three weeks at our church, Ralph ran the youth group, so all of us girls got to spend lots of time with him. A few days after he went back to college, he phoned me and asked me out on a date. I was ecstatic, and just as you would expect from a 15-year-old, I danced and shouted all over the house; my brother Jayden thought I had gone mad. Needless to say, that day I lost my best friend, June - but no matter; I had gained myself a boyfriend. Teenagers are so self-centred! I was besotted. He drove a car, was polite, and was so much older than me. We had a great first date, so respectful was he that he even asked permission before kissing me. And it was a great first kiss, too. The tricky part was, he lived a good two hours away, but he rang me most nights. The phone was attached to the wall - no such things as mobiles in those days - so no other family member had any chance of making phone calls, as I was never off it.

Ralph managed to come visit most weekends; the great romance was on. In hindsight, I realise now that I was so young, besotted and still very much a baby in my faith, so I had no idea what I was walking into. I just kept thinking how pleased God would be, because I had chosen a Bible college student, and was most likely going to become a pastor's wife. I was lost in puppy love, doing whatever he told me to do. It is not possible for a lovestruck teenager to have the wherewithal to recognise the subtleties of manipulation and control. I am not even sure if Ralph even realised, he was doing it - but he sure learnt the craft well. I was so convinced that Victory was in control that I never gave Sinister a thought, but he was most definitely at work. The other issue at this point was that my parents were completely besotted too; they loved him, and because he was a Bible college student, they gave him free rein.

This is an example of the subtle way Ralph approached his manipulation. He would send me letters, listing how many times he had kissed me, and demanding that I needed to start kissing him more; he also kept a record of butt-grabbing that he did, which - to his disapproval - I had not reciprocated. He would send me letters with his demands, and then sign them with "I love you so much, love Ralph," the words written out in tiny little kisses. He demanded, and then signed off with his undying love. The smiling assassin. I was so confused but forced myself to get with the program and shape up. After all, he was the guy God chose for me, wasn't he? I was in that typical, teenage, starry-eyed love phase, while he was a calculating adult who wanted a wife to meet a certain criterion so that it would look good on his church pastor's resume. He told me that it was of utmost importance that I was from the correct side of the Harbour Bridge, I had to dress well, speak well, and never share an opinion; and it was imperative that I was a virgin.

I'm not saying it was all terrible; in fact, our relationship was incredible in many ways. We had a lot of amazing times together, he spoilt me and looked after me, and to add to my dizzy admiration, he even became the church youth leader. What I am trying to portray here though - which of course I didn't realise at the time - was that he was in control of me, even to the point that he was grooming me. I think part of the narcissistic personality is to try to mould and shape a person into their perfect image of who they want you to be. That's what I mean by grooming. That's why I think Ralph chose me. He had his choice of women, but I was the right one because I was young and timid enough to be manipulated.

Six months into our relationship, Ralph wanted to buy me a friendship ring, but before he purchased it, I had to pledge that I had no intention of breaking up with him. It was a way for him to get me to be committed before I was an adult. But I was only 15, I shouldn't have had to make such a promise. I did, though, and with gladness I got my ring - because in my mind, I was going to marry him. And yes, I stood by this promise; I would go on to be engaged at age 17, with plans to marry on Valentine's Day, four days after my 19th birthday.

Despite my devotion and commitment, I was, in Ralph's opinion, still not keeping up my end of the dating criteria; in his view I was 'frigid' - so he hatched a brilliant plan to fix me. He told me that he'd had mumps when he was a child, which meant that he was sterile and unable to have children. He was aware that I looked forward to being a mother one day, so he wanted me to know, so he said, just in case I wanted to end the relationship. I was devastated at the news - not for me but for him. How awful. Always the one to look at the sunny side of life, though, I just said, "Not to worry, we will adopt". Surprise, surprise - a couple of weeks later, in a letter, Ralph revealed that it wasn't true - he just wanted to see if I would stay with him and, his more evil motive, to see if I would be more forward in my sexual advances. Mind you, he didn't want sex - because he knew that a good Christian waits until marriage - but he did want to push the boundaries as far as possible, and I wasn't forthcoming enough. In his mind, he had hatched the perfect plan to fix that. What a manipulative mind. Sadly, I was oblivious. I am telling you, there were times in our make-out sessions that they got very heated, and he would then yell at me, because apparently it was my job, as the girl, to pull the brakes. Such mixed signals.

Let us digress, too many emotions swirling through my head.

My friends all thought Ralph was amazing, as he would show up on a Friday afternoon to pick us all up after school and drive everyone home. This caused issues with the 'cool kids' at school.

The "in" crowd did not appreciate the fact that I had a boyfriend, never mind an older one, and they teased me without mercy. I was tripped, spat upon and called all sorts of names. Teenagers can be so cruel. When I went to school there was no way you would tell a teacher about bullying; you would get your head flushed in the toilet for doing so. Thank God there was no such thing as social media in my day, that would have been a disaster.

At age 17 I was offered a job in the travel industry. In year 10 I did work experience at a travel agent in the city. It was in the MLC building, and I was supposed to go up to Jetstar on floor 17, but I turned up on the ground floor at a travel agent instead. Unbeknownst to me, I turned up and spent a week doing work experience at the wrong place! I was then offered a job there as a junior consultant. The '80s! It seems that fate, or more to the point, Victory, was smiling on me, helping me to get a start. Mind you, one of my bosses would dictate letters while smoking and chewing on his cigarette butt in front of me, while my other boss had incontinence issues and smelt like urine. I was earning $90 a week, and spending most of it on the train trips. They would flirt and be inappropriate and I never questioned it. But I had my foot in the door. I worked there for a year before getting a job locally. Even though I wanted to be a social worker, Ralph had made it very clear that he would not wait for me to finish university. He didn't want a girlfriend who was always studying. So, being the submissive girlfriend, I'd learnt to be, I quit school, and started work.

I must tell you what happened to my horse, Zapp. This was one of many occasions where I was ordered to choose between Ralph and something else, I loved - this time, it was Zapp. I was sixteen at the time, and my doting boyfriend, jealous of the time I was spending with my horse, demanded that I send Zapp away. He was sent to a farm a few hours away; how wonderful - now I could devote all my spare time to Ralph. Tragically though, within a couple of weeks of the move, Zapp escaped his paddock, and was galloping down the road in the middle of the night when he was struck by a truck. He died trying to make it home. Another horse of mine had passed away. I vowed at the time never to get another horse, but that didn't stick for too long - because if you know horses, then you know how special the bond is. It's not something you ever really leave behind.

Ralph and I were very involved in our church, and together we ran the youth group. I have some great memories of this time: ten pin bowling nights, car rallies, ice-skating, progressive dinner, loads of fun. We also went on as many church family camps as we could possibly find. It was a way to spend time together as a group, but in a safe and fun environment. We couldn't get ourselves into too much trouble, as the girls' dormitories were separate to the boys. There was one camp where, at breakfast after our first night, all the young men were laughing and snickering. Supposedly Ralph was a sleep talker and while asleep he had said, "Mmm, nice warm bum you have." I was so embarrassed, and I went bright red, as happened so easily.

During these camps, everyone played pranks on each other, so it was no surprise to find your bed short-sheeted or to find that the milk you were pouring over your cereal was in fact half shaving cream. The favourite, a classic old prank, was to put glad wrap over the toilet bowl so that when the guys went to pee in the middle of the night, it was an unholy mess. Church camps were a lot of fun and a great way to meet new people. I also ended up becoming great friends with Ralph's brother. We had the same wicked sense of humour but unlike me, who lacked the required confidence, he followed through on his pranks. He ended up becoming a member of our church and would often stay at my house when he needed to come to our area. He ended up marrying one of the girls from the youth group and they are still very happily married. We are still friends to this day.

As a couple, in front of others, Ralph and I looked so shiny and perfect - which is exactly what he was going for. Meanwhile, when it was just the two of us, there was a totally different picture going on. One night he had fallen asleep while we were watching a movie, and when he woke up, he assumed I was mad at him. So, the next day, he didn't pick me up as planned. I waited all day for him, and eventually mum came home and asked where he was. I had no idea – and of course in those days there was no such thing as mobile phones. Mum panicked, because that's what my mum did, saying, "Oh no, he has been in a car accident! There's no way he would just not show up." I took on mum's panic and began freaking out. Mum and I drove down to where he was staying but couldn't find him. I was so worried that I rang the local hospital, but of course he wasn't there either. Next day, he sauntered in and informed me that he'd simply spent the day asleep at home, as I needed to be punished for being angry at him.

Hopefully at this point you, dear reader, are shaking your head in disbelief. I sure am. I was so young and naive and couldn't see the manipulation that was unfolding in front of me. As far as I was concerned, this was how all relationships were.

Around this time my parents sold our house, so I decided not to move with them, but instead moved in with a friend and her mum. I was such a grown-up, engaged to be married, and I wanted to experience living out of home before marriage. I enjoyed this season. I had lots of friends coming over, and it was nice to have that bit of independence. One of the friends who stayed with us made the mistake of being a male. Ralph, being very jealous and possessive, accused my male friend of trying to steal me. It made things very unpleasant, and I had to constantly reassure him that nothing was going on. Ralph was always keeping a close eye on me, making sure I did not spend too much time with other males. I just thought he was just looking out for me. If only I'd realised then, how controlling he was.

I should also mention in this chapter that my younger brother Jayden was only 10 years old when Ralph started dating me, which made Ralph 10 years his senior. Despite their 10-year age gap, Ralph spent a fair amount of time with my little brother, which I maybe would have questioned at the time if I had been more aware. I would now go as far as saying that Jayden was also being groomed in so far as Ralph was manipulating him to be his little protege. He was very influenced by Ralph, and in the future, he would idolise all that Ralph became involved with. Because of his older friend's influence, he has made many wrong decisions in his life. Yet they are still close friends to this day.

Despite the red flags that I failed to see, Ralph and I were married, just after I turned 19 - on February 14, Valentine's Day. It was a lovely wedding, but it certainly had its hiccups, starting before the ceremony even began. The vintage Rolls Royce, which was meant to deliver me to the church on time, got a flat tyre. It took over 40 minutes to fix, making me very late. Ralph was not impressed. It was a hot summer's day and he had wanted the whole Olde-English shebang, dressed up to the nines in top hat, tails and gloves. As for me, I wore the typical puffy white gown of the '80s, while my bridesmaids wore white hats and gloves with their puffy crimson Laura Ashley dresses. While it looked impressive, in hindsight it was way too much for a sweltering Australian summer.

The Rolls Royce incident wasn't our only wedding calamity. At the reception, the waitress dropped beetroot on my dress. It goes without saying that if you're going to have food dropped on your wedding dress, you'd choose anything but the beetroot. Then, after the reception, at the moment we were due to leave in style, Ralph realised he had forgotten the keys to our escape vehicle, my restored VW Beetle. We had to wait in the scorching sun with all our guests, while someone went on a key-finding mission. As if all of that wasn't enough drama, the finishing touch was that our honeymoon destination had been wiped out by a cyclone a couple of weeks earlier. We persevered with our honeymoon plans and went there anyway. While our venue was liveable, the township had been decimated and there was rubbish and debris everywhere. Perhaps I should have stopped at the time and wondered why all of this was happening. Lovestruck as we were, though, none of these things bothered us. I had ticked all his boxes, managing to submit to his authority, present myself correctly in public, and become the picture-perfect bride. To top Ralph's cake with icing, I had even started singing lessons and was now singing in church: the ideal ministry role for a soon-to-be pastor's wife. We had dated for four years, we had finally made it to the altar, and Ralph finally gets the sex he has so patiently waited for. Nothing untoward about that at the time - but little did I know what a preoccupation this was to become for him.

When we returned from our honeymoon, we settled into a quaint little granny flat right on the water. I slipped easily into new-wife persona, enjoying having guests over, and experimenting in the kitchen. One embarrassing night after we had made love, we were walking around our flat naked, when one of our male friends came a-knocking. We had a glass door, so everyone got a fright. I was so embarrassed – but Ralph and our visitor both thought it was hilarious. I would have been grateful if the ground had opened up and swallowed me then and there.

Being Christians of the '80s, we were very conservative; you didn't discuss sex with anyone. Today it seems that is all people talk about. It amazes me how society changes. It makes me wonder, are we more enlightened now, or have we gone too far the other way? Sex today is more like a sport, hooking up when you first meet someone. I think it ruins the wonder of it all, taking it slow, spending time with each other, making sure you are compatible. Saving yourself for that special someone. I believe there is a spiritual connection, a soul tie, that occurs with every sexual partner you have, and when that relationship dissolves, it is very hard to sever that tie. It can cause a lot of anguish, and it makes sense that recovering from a breakup can take a huge emotional toll.

But Ralph and I, we were - for the most part - sublimely happy, ready to launch into our happily-ever-after lives. Here was I, thinking Victory had supremacy, but Sinister was never far away. Even when you believe you have done everything right, the walls can still come tumbling down.

Chapter 4

NEWLY WEDS

RALPH AND I settled into married life. It all seemed that our path forward was clear, and we would go into the ministry shortly - the pastor and his wife. For the time being, I continued to work in the travel industry and got myself a job closer to home. Ralph was a qualified panel beater and now a graduate college student. He wasn't interested in repairing cars, though, and instead decided to become a life insurance agent. He was very gifted at sales and became one of the top salespeople, and as a reward we were sent on a fancy cruise.

On this cruise, there was a lot of pressure on me to present myself well; I had to dress appropriately and socialise to his standards. This was tricky as I was terrible at small talk and lacked confidence, and when I felt awkward, I would say too much or nothing at all. I also had the misfortune of glowing red when embarrassed. There were many situations when I knew he wasn't pleased with me in front of others and my face would turn crimson. It made it so hard for me to enjoy any social gathering amongst his business peers. I didn't have an issue with church friends, as I was very comfortable with them, and Ralph tolerated my silly behaviour around them. My personality is actually quite bubbly, fun, and joyful. I love to laugh and play jokes on people. When I am around people I know and love, I'm at ease and I have all the confidence in the world. The problem was, there were many occasions when I was placed on display for Ralph, in front of those I didn't know, and I failed him miserably. He often told me that I was an embarrassment and I lacked confidence, because my parents never encouraged me to be confident in who I am. He found it easy to lay blame. The problem is, it's not so much what my parents didn't do - but what my husband did do. He constantly belittled me, and constantly expected me to behave in a way he deemed proper. It was him who made me lack confidence, because as I matured, our relationship took its toll: I had become scared to show the actual personality that God gave me.

We went to his parents' place one afternoon and I remember I had said something inappropriate, and he kicked me under the table. His parents thought I didn't have an opinion because I never spoke. I was constantly watching what I said and how I should behave. The times we went over there were excruciating, and I would go home exhausted from trying so hard.

Despite all of this we were nevertheless in a very happy season. We managed to go away on a few amazing holidays, thanks to me being in the travel industry. When we travelled on these trips we had a great time, as there was no pressure placed on my performance. Ralph was all about looking good in front of others - so while we were on holidays and had no audience, he didn't have to put on the big show. He could relax and we could just enjoy our time together. If only we could always be on holidays.

One of these trips was to India. Ralph's parents had lived in India when he was young, and they had always encouraged him to be a missionary over there. So, we went on a fact-finding mission to see how we could live successfully in India. It did not go well, and I have never been back. Maybe if I ever get the chance to go back, I will do it differently: five-star, luxury. As it was, on our trip we were young and inexperienced and assumed things would work. Why wouldn't public transport be a good way to get from A to B? Our dramas started in Delhi, where you would grab a rickshaw and ask to be taken to a certain place - but would end up somewhere entirely different. After much arguing you would then arrive at your destination, where you were expected to pay an overcharged fee. There was no point in refusing to pay, they had nowhere else to be so they were quite content to gesticulate endlessly until you were exhausted. Ralph did not tolerate this behaviour and would argue vehemently. We were talking about a few dollars - why the angst? After Delhi, we hopped on a train to the north where we were meeting a pastor who was a friend of Ralph's family. Three hours on the train should have been pleasant enough. Alas, we shared a cabin with three businessmen, who proceeded to ask many questions. When they found out we had been married for nearly three years, I was scorned. How dare I not give my husband a baby? It was my duty as his wife to produce an heir. No amount of reasoning helped my case; I was remonstrated with for the entire train trip. This was just the beginning when it comes to how Indian men treated me. Whenever I was on a train, I was stared at, and groped.

After spending a week with this pastor and their church, where Ralph preached and I sang, we travelled - by bus this time - across the border to Nepal. The Nepalese were a lot friendlier, a complete contrast. We climbed the mountains in a bus, and the roads were not what I would call roads, rather mountain tracks with room for only one car. All through the night the bus driver would blast the horn to warn oncoming traffic we were coming at them. What was said to be a 'pothole' was closer to a crater. It was a scary ride where no sleep happened whatsoever. Nevertheless, we were young and resilient, took it in our stride, and I truly loved Nepal. We travelled into the Chitwan National Park where we went white water rafting, we trekked the Annapurna Range, and we explored the city of Kathmandu.

We had a lovely experience in Nepal - but our time there came to an end, and we had to head back into India via the bus again. Yikes. This time the bus actually broke down and we all climbed into the back of an open truck bed to get back across the border. Talk about adventure. The day we arrived back in India, it was a holy day, and everything was shut. The only thing available to get us to the train station from the border, was a pony cart. Now you would think Ralph, being a gentleman and a recently married one at that, would make me sit up the front with the driver - but no, I was sitting on the back with my legs dangling while he took the prime position up front. We hadn't gone far when a mob of locals swamped the cart. They were all high on 'happy cookies' and painted in bright colours in celebration of their holy day, and they came at me and threw paint on me while groping. I was terrified. The driver of our cart tried his best to push the pony through the crowd. I jumped off and ran as soon as we arrived at the station. I looked a sight, covered in paint where no-one but my husband should have touched. The train was the only other form of transport working that day, and consequently it was full. The conductor kindly, for a fee, offered us his cabin. We were so relieved as we could close the cabin door and catch up on sleep. It had been over two days of travelling. I was on the top bunk and fell into an exhausted sleep. Mistakenly, I thought I was safe. I was wrong. While I slept the conductor came in and put his hands down my pants. I screamed; he ran. Needless to say, that was the end of my sleep. How on earth was I going to live in a place like this?

The next issue we had was hunger: we had not eaten since leaving Kathmandu two days prior. You did not buy street food back then - it was considered unsafe for our unaccustomed, Western stomachs - but there were no restaurants open. We managed to find some mandarins and had to survive on those until we finally arrived at the next church. The beautiful wife of the pastor quickly made us breakfast which we devoured, but unfortunately it hit our stomachs and bounced back. Too many Indian spices!

At the end of this visit we were headed back home, and I was very much looking forward to it, as was Ralph. I might have had issues with the local men, but he had issues with the food - he had 'India belly' for the entire trip. He also found it hard to communicate with the local church leaders; he was very set in his ways, as were the pastors. He clashed with them constantly on church policies and doctrine. India was not the place for us. 'Become missionaries' was scratched off our to do list.

At age 21, I decided to take a year off work and attend a creative arts college for singing and song writing. I love to learn, and this was the perfect time for me to do it, while Ralph was doing well in business and there were no babies. It was a great year, a lot of fun, and although I realised the gift of song writing had not been bestowed upon me, I excelled in singing. During this year I still worked part time in travel, and I was offered a work trip to Bali, which I took during college holidays. Whilst I was away Ralph started hanging out with one of my female college friends. He wasn't answering my calls or contacting me while I was away, and when I returned, he was very late collecting me from the airport. When he finally showed he was with my friend, and they were flirting and being inappropriate. Alarm bells went off - I was very concerned. The two of them spent a lot of time together but I didn't know what to do about it. It was no doubt all in my head, I told myself. I had no evidence of anything actually happening, and I was quite sure nothing did take place - but that does not mean it wasn't something to be aware of. My friend eventually quit college and became an escort. Suspicious? I think so. She dropped out of our lives after that, and to this day I still have no idea if anything happened between them.

After college I went back to work full time as a travel consultant. It is a very rewarding job and being able to travel is a great bonus. The pay is terrible - but the payoff is that the benefits are great. We would try to travel as much as possible and took advantage of cheap flights and accommodation. Ralph was doing well with insurance and in this season, it would seem that Victory was taking a stand.

When I was 22, we purchased our first house. Interest rates were out of control at 18% but because Ralph was in insurance, we were able to secure a home loan for 8%. We were very blessed to be able to buy a home at such a young age. It was a delightful little cottage, and I took great pleasure in decorating. There were a lot of overgrown weeds and bushes out the back, so we decided to have two goats join us - Hooley and Dooley. This was the start of what would become quite a menagerie of animals over the years. These goats did what they were asked to do: clear the land - but they also loved to visit us inside and their favourite thing was jumping on the bed. Goats are a great pet, but they do not know how to behave! The neighbours were not too happy with our goats as they often visited them too, uninvited.

The following year our first daughter was born, Harmony. Ralph really wanted a girl and when she was born, he was over the moon. He was a great father when she was young. I went back to travel on a casual basis, and I remember when Harmony was eighteen months old, I was offered a work trip. Ralph insisted I take it; he was more than happy to stay home with Harmony for the week. If you were to look at our happy family at that time you would see that all looked great, we appeared happy, and Victory was in control. Unfortunately, Sinister is never too far away, and looks for many opportunities to undermine. All was good as long as I behaved correctly.

This first house we lived in was on a very busy road and we had a couple of incidents where our friends' children would escape onto the road. We realised that as Harmony got older it would be risky to stay here, so we decided to sell. We moved to a beautiful Queenslander house complete with bullnose verandah and high ceilings. It was charming but needed work. Not long after we moved in, Melody was born. Harmony was three months away from turning three and she was so excited to have a baby sister; Ralph not so happy. He wanted a boy and never really accepted the fact that it didn't happen. He did bond with Melody though, and again was a great father to her during the early years - but it wasn't part of his perfect plan. Our lives started to crack, Sinister was on the move.

When I was seven months pregnant with Melody, we had travelled to the Ukraine to visit a friend, and then to Israel and Egypt for a holiday. I loved Israel. It was fascinating seeing the history in this land, to walk where Jesus walked and to go out on the Sea of Galilee. I could live here easily enough. The bible became alive. To experience the places of such historical significance and to walk in the footsteps of Jesus left me speechless. Harmony was having a great time, climbing over ruins, and living on dates and apricots. She took everything in her stride and adapting to all the places we went. After a particularly gruelling day traipsing the old town of Jerusalem, she was so tired she fell fast asleep whilst taking her bath. We had worn her out! Jerusalem is a place where you need to have the time to just sit and watch the people, so many different cultures coming to one city to immerse themselves in the culture of an ancient, holy place. Meandering through the alleyways, stopping at the little shopfronts selling all sorts of trinkets. Harmony was in retail heaven and was fascinated with all the colours and scents before her. It is a city of untold beauty and a sacredness that can't be described in words. Definitely a case of seeing is believing.

After our time in Israel, we boarded a bus to Egypt. We were young and cheap, so 10 hours on a luxury coach seemed reasonable however, this was a time when tourist buses between Israel and Egypt were being targeted by terrorists. A bus only the day before was bombed along the same highway we were travelling. We had no fear though, we believed angels were looking after us and nothing would harm us. We did make it without incident unless you count the crazy two-year-old we had with us who was bored and needed to run around. Oh, the joys of travelling with toddlers.

In Egypt we of course went and explored the pyramids, Harmony loved all the steps into the interiors of them. She had small enough feet to climb the many steps meanwhile her very pregnant mother had to go nice and slow. We went to the grand bazaar in Cairo and were offered 10,000 camels in exchange for Harmony. We declined as we had nowhere to keep that many camels and getting them home would have been a logistical nightmare. Harmony was getting very frustrated in this country, she had lovely blonde hair, which of course is rare in the Middle East, and often people would just grab her, pick her up and kiss her. They would also pin little seeing-eye pendants onto her. After a couple of days, she got quite sick of it and as soon as she saw anyone approaching, she would say "No, do not touch me".

Harmony got tired of hanging out with her parents at one stage and tried to go and holiday with another family. We had boarded a luxury boat to sail down the River Nile to Aswan. Time to just relax and rest. Whilst onboard Harmony found herself a lovely couple and befriended them. She decided that they were going to be her new parents, she wanted to sleep in their cabin and when it came time to go our separate ways, she threw a delightful tantrum and told us she had new parents, we were no longer required. Dragging our distraught daughter away from her 'new parents' was a challenge! Eventually she fell into an exhausted sleep.

Our time in the Middle East was amazing, but while we were travelling, we discussed Ralph starting our own church as an outreach from the one we were currently attending. After all, he was fully qualified, and we definitely had the experience. The idea was to let our pastor know our intentions and then start off by running a home church and then building from there. We returned from our trip and went to see the pastor - but he wasn't happy with our vision. It wasn't what he wanted and he in fact asked us to leave the church and have no more contact with fellow members. I know this sounds crazy, right? And yes, it was - but I understood and was accepting of his decision. Unfortunately, I believe Ralph took it to heart and took deep offence. He walked away from the pastor and all the church members and decided he was going to establish his church, regardless of not receiving any support. Sinister whispered in his ear that he didn't need anyone's help and was quite capable of doing this thing on his own. He became impossible to live with. He started spouting off the view that all traditional churches were institutions that were 'outside of the grace of God'. The true church was found only in small house groups that met weekly, and once a month everyone would gather in a larger group. So, this is the model we now followed. We stopped going to the traditional church and the girls and I came under his spiritual leadership, and his only.

This was his great plan: before starting our first home church, we had to renovate our house to accommodate a large gathering. In fact, as it turned out, our house church would never begin. Ralph decided to build under our house and construction began. But Ralph was working from home as well as doing our renovations and placed an enormous amount of pressure on himself. He had lost interest in selling insurance; after all he wanted to be in ministry even though he no longer believed in the church in the traditional format. He still wanted to be involved with the administration side of the church. And so, he started to research how to set up a charity - what was needed to start one, what was considered a charity, and what were the benefits. He was very clever and worked out that all churches could benefit from having a registered charity. If the church set up a soup kitchen, an op shop, a counselling arm, or anything that benefitted the community, it could receive charity status. It really was a great opportunity that enabled a lot of community-based churches that didn't have a lot of funds to assist and help a broad range of people. This enabled churches to operate tax free and purchase a car for the use of the charity, without having to pay the luxury sales tax and Government costs. It is all a bit confusing for me, to be honest. But Ralph had hit a goldmine. Our house church never began, and this venture took over.

Ralph rang churches far and wide offering his expertise in setting up their charity and organising a brand-new car for them. Pastors were so grateful, as up until this time most churches only had members volunteering to look after the needy. Pastors were generally on very low wages, often working outside of the church, and when they were told they could actually drive a new car and claim it as a tax benefit, many pastors organised for Ralph to purchase a car for them. There was nothing illegal about this, but the issue was, this set-up allowed Ralph to funnel money into his own pocket. When he was running low on funds, he would organise to buy a car on behalf of one of his charities for a very discounted rate, and then after he had driven it for a couple of months, he would sell it back to the car dealer close to the amount of the original sales price. He would then pocket the difference. It was easy money, and of course I benefited because it went towards our living expenses, and I also enjoyed the luxury of driving a new car - but it wasn't right. I was not allowed to question it, as this was met with "it is not your concern, you have no idea about finances and of course it is right, it's for the benefit of our non-profit organisations."

Ralph set up many charities within churches and the churches were doing the right thing by providing for their local communities. Ralph, on the other hand, didn't have a church, but he did set up charities and non-profits to suit his own personal needs. He wasn't under anyone's leadership so he could do whatever he wanted and not only that, but pastors also loved him. He was a gift to the local churches, and he became their golden boy. He was full of pride and became even harder to live with.

He then went on to research Government grants and he discovered another lucrative loophole. He applied for a grant that was offering a large sum of money for a charity to organise people to visit the elderly in nursing homes, who weren't receiving any visitors. He contacted the local churches and organised for volunteers from the church to visit the elderly. They, being charitable and happy to help, would gladly visit the nursing homes and Ralph kindly offered to pay for any expenses like food, treats or flowers, and their petrol to get to and from the nursing home. They received a pittance compared to the thousands he received from the grant. Again, I was not allowed to question him on this. It was a few years before the Government started to crack down on charities/non-profits, and started to audit funds, and this stream of money started to dry up. It wasn't long before Ralph would find a new avenue to make money - he was never cashless for long.

While all this was going on and Ralph was working from home, it was not a pleasant environment. I was working casually in travel, but there wasn't a lot of work, so we were both at home a lot. Even though I was busy raising toddlers, I was told I was lazy and that all I did was read books. I had to account for my day by writing on a whiteboard a list of all the housework I had done. It was frowned upon if I went out with friends, but so long as the house was clean, the girls well behaved and the dinner cooked I was allowed to socialise with friends from church. Ralph also constantly told me I wasn't allowed to get fat like his mother, it would not be tolerated, so make sure I ate in moderation. I was a size ten up until I had the children, and then I began to sneak up to a size 12. Ralph's mother unfortunately was very overweight, but I didn't have her genes, so why would he even think that it was even possible for me. He was so egotistical.

I wasn't enjoying being at home and always being criticised, so I did the most logical thing possible (not really): I decided to go into business with my mum. Melody was two years old when my indoor play centre, Little Munchkins, was launched. I went from a stay-at -home mum, to working full time including weekends. Now I couldn't be criticised for being lazy.

LITTLE MUNCHKINS

LITTLE MUNCHKINS WAS launched when I was 28 years old. Mum and I found a warehouse and we painted it in bright, bold colours. Watching the construction of the playground was so exciting. We had a massive ball pit, a speed slide, a spiral slide, a mini flying fox, tunnels, and platforms to climb. We also designed a toddler area with a mini ball pit and things appropriate for the under-twos, and we added a toy library, which enabled people to take toys home on loan. And of course, the centre wasn't complete without a café, which would serve the parents food and drinks while their children played.

We were set up and raring to go. There were only a couple of other indoor playgrounds in Australia and neither of them had all that we had. I was no longer going to be accused of being lazy, we were open seven days a week as well as Friday nights. I had this business for seven years and it was one of the hardest things I have ever done. I was in for a huge learning curve, with many Victory moments and many Sinister moments as well, along the way.

Little Munchkins was a high-pressure environment. We had approximately 17 casual staff ranging from teens to my mum's age. Little Munchkins could have up to 60 screaming children at any one time, under the age of 12, and parents had to stay and supervise as it wasn't a childcare facility. Some of the parents at the café were so demanding; they would order their skim latte, decaf double mochaccino, or babycino, and if it wasn't delivered within moments they would carry on as if the world was ending. You can imagine how many coffee orders we had to do all at once when there were up to sixty children in attendance. It was hard to stay calm; jugs of milk were lined up and coffees delivered to tables as quickly as possible, which was in itself fraught with fear as you had to navigate to the tables through any number of running children. You will be pleased to know that not one coffee landed on a child in all those years.

We wanted the cafe side of things to serve delicious food so that the parents also had a lovely experience. I can still recall the smell of popcorn and to this day do not enjoy eating it. There was no time limit in the playground and café, so often dads would come in on a Saturday morning with their children and their newspaper and stay all day. I am sure they went home bragging to their wives how they looked after the children all day and gave her a delightful day off. So long as it was a sunny day (when it wasn't too chaotic), we loved it when the fathers came in - as they spent so much money on food trying to make sure the children were happy.

Rainy days were out of control; people would be lining up to come in. It was a war zone. The hardest part was when we were full to capacity and had to turn people away. People were not happy, but there was nothing that could be done and as we had no time limit, we couldn't ask people to leave, they were free to stay all day. Mind you, if I was a customer, I would never have chosen to stay all day in the chaos myself, a couple of hours to let the children run off steam was more than sufficient. On days like this it was all hands on deck, with staff running around making food and coffee, and helping supervise the children. Even though this was really the parents' responsibility, they were often too busy chatting to their friends and sipping on their lattes to pay proper attention to their kids! The toy library would be the last thing you had time to look after, but it was guaranteed everyone wanted to hire something during the busiest moments.

I really don't know how I kept sane during these 7 years, but it is amazing what you are capable of when the need arises. Picture it: 60 excited, screaming children, balls flying everywhere, kids demanding a bag of popcorn, dozens of coffees and milkshakes on back order, making sure the food is served hot and then the worst possible thing happens. A child pees in the ball-pit. The ball-pit must be shut down, (it's everyone's favourite part of the playground), the ball cleaner must be activated, and thousands of balls have to be put through the machine and sterilised. I break out in a sweat even now just thinking about it.

After a couple of years working with mum, we decided to open another playground - we took over another business that had already been established, and mum went off to manage that one. It turned out to be a very bad decision, as the way it had been set up by the previous owners was not good. The playground was too small for the number of tables set up in the cafe. It was more like a cafe with a playground, rather than our model of a playground with a cafe. This business nearly destroyed my mum; she was so stressed and worked ridiculously hard and very long hours. It was impossible to get reliable staff, and the rent and expenses were a lot higher than at my playground. Sinister was destroying her confidence and robbing her financially.

Mum had come to a point of complete exhaustion one night when a child had defecated in the tunnels, and she had to go disinfect and scrub the entire playground. Mum was sobbing and beyond fatigue - and that was when 'Victory' showed up. Mum had a powerful spiritual experience. She describes how Jesus appeared to her in the tunnel. She experienced his love, which renewed her strength and got her through another day. From that day forward my mum fully believed in the resurrection power of Jesus Christ and put aside all the New Age beliefs that were controlling her life. She literally became a new creation, she was more confident and full of joy. Not long after this my parents decided to shut the playground as it was going backwards financially, and no matter how hard my mum worked, it just wasn't worth the stress. They lost a considerable amount of money, but it was the best decision for them.

After this time, I was fully in charge of our original playground, and a typical day at Munchkins would include parties for up to 30 children set up in one section, and the cafe area open to everyone else, as well as the toy library. We would schedule up to four parties on any given day, with the first one set to start at 9am. I have to say that unfortunately many of our staff, especially the young ones, were so unreliable! There was many a time when my young staff members would not show up for work as they'd had a massive night and wanted to sleep it off. I would come in first thing, set everything up for the party, and then start to panic as I had no one to run the party games. Parents didn't take kindly to paying for something they were not going to get. I would be ringing everyone I knew to try get help; mum was not available as my parents had moved an hour away. The one person you are supposed to turn to when you really need them is your spouse. Ralph now had an office literally next door, so he was the logical person to call to come and help. At least until other staff could get there. But he never once came to my rescue. He would always tell me his work was more important than mine, he was the one making all the money, sort it out yourself as it is your problem, not mine. Sinister was loud and clear. I shed a lot of tears over the countless times he rejected my pleas for help. My world was crumbling but I was too busy to do anything about it.

The truth of the matter is that Ralph loved showing off my business to what he classified as important people. He would bring businesspeople in for lunch and brag about how his playground was a non-profit enterprise run by his wife. Here I was operating a business seven days a week without any support from him, and he was using it to not only brag, but also to legitimise his own business.

One of the great benefits of running the business was that my daughters had the privilege of growing up with their own personal playground. I am sure it wasn't always a privilege for them, as they had to share their mother with a lot of people, but it most definitely gave them an incredible amount of life skills. Harmony was at school during this time, and Melody at preschool. The days that Melody was not at preschool, and it was time for her nap, I would set up the portable cot in the back of my van which I parked directly outside where I was working, and she would have her nap between her playtimes. I was very fortunate that she was so easy going and it never bothered her, or maybe it was because she was so exhausted living in a playground that she was happy to sleep in the back of a van. Both my daughters' personalities shone forth while they had Munchkins. We called Harmony the Munchkin police as she always kept an eye on all the children and reported back to us if anyone was misbehaving. Meanwhile Melody was the carer, and if there was a child playing alone, she would make friends. My girls never had time to be bored and I loved the fact that I could run a business while having my children with me. I am not saying it was easy; when I was in the midst of an extremely busy moment you could guarantee that one of the girls would need something. It was hard juggling it all - but we made it work. Victory was an invisible presence that helped smooth the rocky road and the girls had to learn to wait patiently for their mum's attention.

The girls thrived on all the attention from the staff, and they learnt to be great communicators. They were both confident in answering the telephone and would often hand the phone to me as someone on the other end was trying to book a party, not realising they were talking to a four-year-old. On our frantic days I would often leave the girls on front entrance duty, where they would sign people in and collect the entrance fee. They both became excellent at maths. They saw how hard I worked and as a result both have thrived in their chosen professions because of their work ethic. Neither had issues finding jobs when they were teenagers, and they would often be asked to work more than they were able.

I have always been complimented on how well I brought up the girls. The only advice I can give parents is that children learn by example; they are always watching and taking everything in, so be very much aware about the way you conduct yourself and treat others, always be kind. It is also imperative that you do not ignore your children; if they are trying to get your attention do all you can to stop and allow them to communicate their needs. Communication in any relationship is the key to success. There were days when I could not give the girls the attention they needed but I would always stop what I was doing, look them in the eyes, apologise and let them know that as soon as it was possible I would look after their needs. I made sure to always follow through on this promise. I never made a promise if I knew I could not follow through on it. They never forget when a promise is broken. And sadly, in the coming years there were so many instances when Ralph did not follow through on his promises to them.

The girls also learnt to eat fancy food growing up, as I definitely didn't have the time to have fussy eaters. They ate what we made at the café: Caesar salads and spicy nachos; focaccia with toppings like eggplant, capsicum, sun-dried tomatoes, or chicken, avocado and mozzarella, or turkey, brie and cranberry. Their palettes were set for life and they both now enjoy eating out and experiencing all kinds of different cuisines.

Another way the girls entertained themselves was to load up a game on the computer. They were only allowed to play educational games for subjects like spelling, maths and geography but really, they didn't know there were other options anyway, and were content to play these. I am convinced this is one of the reasons Melody excelled in school as she was learning way before she even attended school. This is definitely Victory at work as I had no idea about the importance of teaching them all these skills while they were young. I was at a job that allowed them to be involved and consequently they learnt life skills, communication skills and learning skills by default. 'Victory' did just as much parenting of them as I did! While I was busy in the kitchen, they were busy learning grammar and math equations, or making new friends on the playground.

The girls had the absolute best birthday parties. Their entire class would be invited, which meant they received up to 30 birthday presents. They didn't care less about the location, the presents were the prize, especially for Harmony, as gifts was her number one love language. Little Munchkins was known to be the place to have your party, and when you received an invite, it was the best. When my girls received an invite from a friend, it was like their friend had invited them to have a party at their own place. And for seven years I did not need to worry about organising a party for them. The party organised itself.

After a couple of years in business we came up with the concept of a Friday night disco. We opened this up for children up to 15 years old, and it was only for birthday parties. We would clean up after the daytime play sessions, and then set the place up for anywhere up to three parties, turn off the lights, put spotlights on the playground, and coloured disco lights on the dance floor. We had a professional DJ who would lead them all in the Nutbush and anything Spice Girls. This was a huge success, and you had to book your party months in advance. It was so much fun that I wanted to have a birthday party there myself!

I do have a memory of one of my birthdays; it had been a particularly busy day and the girls just wanted to celebrate with me. Unfortunately, though, all my staff abandoned me for other commitments, and I was left alone to finish up at work: sterilise the equipment, sweep and mop the floor, clean the kitchen and the coffee machine. In other words, a lot of work. The girls were disappointed as they wanted to go out to celebrate, so they rang their dad to ask if he could come help. His response was, "I'm busy". I think we all had a cry. My mum and brother ended up coming to help and then we all went out for dinner without Ralph. His work was way more important than his wife's birthday. I knew this and did not expect it to be any other way.

Even though this was an extremely challenging business it was also very rewarding. It kept me very focused and unable to spend a lot of time worrying about what Ralph was up to. I made many friends and became very well known in the community. It was important to me that I handled everything with total integrity, especially the finances. The taxation office came to audit me one year and I showed him all my books which I kept strictly up to date and correct. After he went through them, he asked how much cash I pocketed. I was so offended that he would even suggest that, but supposedly I am unusual for not putting some cash in my pocket. I think I told him I did no such thing, but I could not guarantee that some of my staff may have helped themselves. The majority of my staff were young, and it is very tempting to see cash in a cash register and not help yourself to a little bit. It is the price you pay as a business owner. Do not get me wrong, I loved my staff, and we were one big happy family - but temptation does happen.

After seven years things started to change. Liability insurance tripled and became cripplingly expensive. Although Little Munchkins looked like a thriving business, it wasn't any longer. I had to maintain a lot of staff, so wages were high; the entrance fee was only $5 for unlimited time, and when the weather was beautiful parents took their children to the park. We were able to cover costs but there was nothing left over. This of course made it easy for Sinister to tell me I was a useless businesswoman and for Ralph to always use the excuse that his business, which was supposedly making, or going to make a fortune, was far superior to mine. It was no surprise that my landlord and Ralph had many a run-in; two hot heads butted up against each other. Our landlord decided that as soon as the lease was up, he was going to shut us down. And that is exactly what happened. He doubled our rent, so with the insurance and the rent-hike, we had no choice but to shut our doors. I contacted the local church and offered everything to them: the playground, the cafe equipment, everything except the toy library. I asked for $30,000 even though it was worth well over $100,000, but the playground had to be dismantled, and fast, because the landlord wanted his building back. The church decided to take everything, and I was so ecstatic that the playground would continue, in a new location, to give children happiness and fun.

I decided to use the money from the sale to take us all to Kenya and Tanzania. It was a reward for the girls for having to share me with the rest of the community for so many years.

While we were away, I asked a close friend's husband to paint the warehouse back to basic white, and I told her the church would be organising to have the playground dismantled and everything moved out. Upon our return from Africa the church contacted me very distraught as I had given them a list of all the things they would be getting, but when they went to pack it all up there were a few items missing. I had no idea what had happened. Guess what - my supposed close friend had decided to help herself. She had taken all the disco equipment, including $2000 worth of CDs, and some cafe equipment. One of the staff from the church went over to her place and found it all in her garage. When he confronted her about it, she said she was worried it might have gotten stolen, so she was kindly 'looking after it' for me. Strange thing is, she only took the black and white chairs; not the red, blue, and yellow ones. She was picky about what she thought might have been stolen. Unfortunately, when owning a business, it is expected that people steal from you. They see you as wealthy and believe they are entitled to some of that wealth. As a large majority of my business was dealing in cash, I have no doubt that staff often helped themselves. Even though my girls were so young, I was better off having them on the front counter than a staff member. It is a sad fact of life.

Chapter
6

RALPH CAPERS & LITTLE MUNCHKINS

WHILE I WAS busy with the girls and Little Munchkins Ralph started to look at alternative money-making ideas. The government had started to tighten rules and make things more difficult in the grant and charity department, and Ralph was starting to dislike all things church. The institution, he believed, was full of hypocrites, and none of them knew their scripture as well as him. We didn't go to church for nine years, and if the girls and I went to a service somewhere, he made it very uncomfortable for us. Maybe I should have gone anyway, but it wasn't really viable when I worked most Sundays. I never lost my faith, and I know God used Victory over this season otherwise, I don't believe I would have survived it.

Meanwhile Ralph was researching and renovating our home, and he became impossible to live with. The girls and I would come home from Little Munchkins and before we were allowed to speak to him, he needed to take two headache tablets, washed done with scotch. Once that had taken effect, we were permitted to share about our day. When Little Munchkins was two years old, and I had turned 30, I concluded I was no longer prepared to put up with Ralph's hateful, controlling ways, and after 11 years of pain I decided to leave him for the first time. I packed up the girls and went to stay with family. I had had enough. During my stay, which was only a few days, Ralph sent me emails telling me all the things I had done wrong, and that I needed to repent and get myself and his girls back home. He explained how I was never interested in sex, and that my upbringing had destroyed my self-confidence. He wanted to make it clear that he had never made a mistake, and he never would. He knew exactly who he was and told me to study King Solomon from the Bible, as that was who he was like in personality. The wisest king that ever lived. He even told me to ask his father as he would be able to confirm that he had done no wrong. He told me he was one of the best negotiators and salesmen around. He was one of the best in manipulation and creating an environment to get what he wanted. He never failed at anything, and he wasn't about to fail at his marriage. He mentioned several times in the emails that the only way to fix our marriage was sex and lots of it. Sinister was having a field day. Please don't cringe at this, but I was so battle weary; I'd had

11 years of varying degrees of this kind of verbal abuse. I was so convinced that divorce was not an option, and that God would never forgive me for such a sin. I just couldn't find the strength to leave permanently. I went back and humbled myself. He forgave me for my foolishness, so long as I realised, he had never done anything wrong. Life did improve for a couple of months, if I was humble and Ralph had his way - but it wasn't long before he was once again doing his life and I was doing mine, with not much meeting in the middle. I would struggle for another five years before I did leave permanently.

I am now going to attempt to explain the new endeavour Ralph discovered. This latest did not involve churches, but it did involve a lot of seminars and training, or more precisely, brain washing. The concept goes something like this: you invested a large sum of money in Ralph's company, which you could claim as a tax deduction because he labelled it non-profit. He would then send these funds overseas, guaranteeing a return of around 10 per cent per week. "Impossible!" I hear you say, but not according to Ralph. Remember, he was an arch manipulator; he was so good at convincing you that no one ever doubted him. People were dropping off bags of money thinking they were going to strike it rich. Ralph went into money overdrive; we were going to be extremely wealthy along with all those who invested. I never understood what was going on, but everyone involved was convinced this venture was legit and an absolute winner. I remember one day a person dropped off a brown paper bag with sixty thousand dollars, their entire savings. Ralph was supposed to then bank this and send it offshore to Vanuatu before it was sent to somewhere else in the world. This money, I am very sorry to say, never went to a bank - he used it to pay for our renovations. When I questioned him, I was given some complicated explanation about how we needed the money, so instead of pulling it out of our investment he would use this, and then transfer the money we had invested into this person's investment. Goodness woman, it isn't that hard to understand. Needless to say, they never saw their money again.

The business went something like this: the banks make billions of dollars on the one and two cent amounts in your bank account, which doesn't get accounted for, they get rounded down. What this scheme supposedly did was plug into these billions of dollars which enabled this ridiculously high return. Totally easy to understand, yes? We were all sucked into this vortex. It was highly successful for a couple of years, clearly because there was a steady stream of willing and deluded investors, just like with every other pyramid scheme out there. If the earlier investors wanted their money the latest investors' money was used to pay them back. It was rare for people to ask for their money back as supposedly the longer it was invested, the higher the return. Ralph didn't actually run this scheme; it was managed through an overseas investment company. Therefore, he was often getting on a plane to Singapore or Hong Kong to meet up with these people. They worked the same way as Ralph, if Ralph wanted his money back from them, they would use the latest investors' money. Obviously, this couldn't go on forever and it started to crumble. Money was not returning as promised from these overseas investors, and they became extremely difficult to contact and to find. Fancy that.

Ralph managed to trace some of our money through a series of banks which sent us off on a journey around the world with only three days' notice. I had to organise staff for Little Munchkins and ask my mum to look after the girls. It was no easy feat, and the girls were not impressed. I committed the trip to God and prayed Victory would be with us, but at the end of the chase it was clearly Sinister taking the lead.

We travelled across countries including Singapore, Germany and finally Israel. No time for jet lag; straight to work.

Diary entry:

DAY 1 - We go to the bank to organise the opening of an account to facilitate the transfer of the stolen funds. Clearly, we were believing for a quick miracle, but no money is transferred.

DAY 2 - We have an appointment with our newly appointed lawyers, we drive up the road to Haifa, meet with them and try to explain what has been going on and why we were stupid enough in the first place to believe this financial scam. Four hours later they are happy to represent us, we just needed to transfer ten thousand dollars as a retainer. Not sure where that is supposed to come from.

DAY 3 - We are now trusting God to supply us with ten thousand dollars before our lawyer becomes suspicious to the fact that we can't pay. Anyway, we meet with them for another day to go over things very slowly. Ten hours later and we are still here, we had to sit in the conference room for hours, no food just coffee. The lawyers are super excited, no not about us, but about their coffee machine, it was a Nescafé bar. This law firm is the biggest in Israel, with many many staff, and every time you pass anyone, they tell you about the coffee machine and ask if I would like a coffee. We stay in this conference room all day, very modern but the chairs were rock hard and my butt was protesting something fierce. While I was sitting there trying to sort this nightmare out the wall next to the conference room moves, oh man was I freaked out. It turns out the wall is a massive movable filing cabinet. My jumping out of my skin reaction must have made them think I was crazy. During our meeting we contact a private investigator, the bank and the police. The PI finds out that the money is stashed at the bank, as we suspected, so it was definitely worth pursuing. Our lawyer then jumps on the phone to the bank to see if we can go open our account. Well actually no – they'd had a phone call from someone in Toronto stating that if an Aussie guy shows up, do not open an account for him. Needless to say, the bank did not approve us. This means war to Ralph. We are treading on toes, so we are closing in. At 6pm we decide to visit the police station in Tel Aviv. Many plain-clothes police officers waiting for us. Let me paint you a picture: At this falling-down, in-bad-repair police headquarters, we go up many stairs through many corridors and arrive at the detective's office. White-washed walls, brown vinyl chairs, brown veneer desktops. I have to say though, the chairs were more comfortable than the lawyers. Another two hours explaining this complicated fraud case. A couple of the police got a bit heated; they believe it is an international matter not local, but our lawyer insists we want it handled and reported in Israel. It had to happen while sitting in a closed room. A detective lights up a cigarette and blows it directly my way. I try to be strong and not cover my mouth or cough. I handled it, but only just. The police hand us over a copy of the report which they are not supposed to do, it was in Hebrew, but it was good to have a copy. It is now 10pm, we grab a bite to eat and then fall into an exhausted sleep.

DAY 4 - *There is not much more our lawyer can do until we file complaints against all the people involved worldwide. We decide to spend the day in Jerusalem with a friend of ours that went to Bible college with Ralph. I praise God that we had a least one day to enjoy this great holy land. We meandered through the marketplace; we traipsed up to the tomb where Jesus was laid and then to the wailing wall. We went and prayed at the wall, a very sacred moment. Thousands upon thousands have prayed at this wall, it was an honour to be able to do the same. It was a precious moment.*

Shabbat was about to start; the sun was on its way down. The Jewish people were about to close shop, not drive a car, or even turn on a light. It is a time to go to the temple and honour God. We decide to go for a drive to Bethlehem and Hebron before driving back to our friend's apartment to celebrate Shabbat. We celebrate with communion. We had a lovely evening and didn't get back to our hotel until after midnight. Another long day but a very worthwhile one. A day in Jerusalem is not enough,

I could spend months here and still not experience everything.

DAY 5 - *Ralph was checking emails and he received one from one of the men we were tracking down. It was slightly intimidating saying he would sue the pants off us if we rocked the boat. We didn't take it all negatively as our thoughts were, at least he was finally communicating with us. We are hoping an arrangement can be made towards getting our funds or a portion of our funds back before it becomes really nasty and really expensive. We are now on our way to London.*

We are zooming through the sky, admiring farmlands, snow-capped mountains and villages, proud of ourselves for booking a flight with a quick one-hour layover in Munich. We were in for a shock; as we made our way to our new gate, we find out that Heathrow, actually the entire UK's navigation system, has crashed. Heathrow, being one of the busiest airports in the world, has planes stacked in the sky waiting to land, at the time of the computer crash many planes were in the air and there were some very close, near misses. Planes were diverted throughout Europe. It was monumental chaos. When you are a frequent traveller, you have to get used to all the delays and mishaps along the way. We were expecting at least a four hour delay, we were fortunate to be one of the last planes out that night with an hour delay to board and a further 90 minute delay on the tarmac. We also had to circle Heathrow for 40 minutes, but we did eventually get there. Customs was in total disarray as they did not have the staff to process all these late-night arrivals, another very late night for us.

DAY 6 - *We declared today a day of rest; it was a Sunday so there wasn't much we could do until another working week started.*

DAY 7 - *We visit a UK lawyer who suggests a civil action against everyone involved. Again, a very costly course of action but probably the most effective way to have the funds returned. Ralph was contemplating staying in London to sort through things, the lawyer was very experienced in these matters and Ralph felt confident working with him. The plan was to send emails to investors asking for financial assistance to fund the civil suit. Interesting how it was Ralph's idea to invest other people's money with these frauds, but he expected them to finance the return of the funds. He decides to not stay as he needed to be back in Australia for other business interests.*

DAY 8 - *We take a drive to the home of the gentleman who was given our funds to see if his castle is worth repossessing. Oh what a dive, a rundown dilapidated place with a beat up old Jag parked out front, certainly nothing I wanted to possess. Ralph believes this is a front, 'Woe is me, I own nothing, it was stolen from me, I have nothing to offer to my investors.' He possibly has properties worldwide.*

DAY 9- *Ralph spends the day catching up on emails, I just relax ready for our evening flight to*

Toronto. Our flight departs on time, and we arrive in Toronto at one in the morning.

DAY 10 - I don't get to explore this city as we are too busy following the money trail. We visit the Ontario Securities Commission, not interested. We have their sympathy but nothing else, they thanked us for drawing their attention to it. Ralph then makes the decision to go visit the gentleman at the top of the food chain, the one that started this investment. His home is spectacular, beautiful and fancy cars to match. We are obviously being entertained in a home financed by our funds and no doubt many others. This gentleman is a smooth talker, better than Ralph. He is extremely sympathetic about our plight; he promises he is working extensively in trying to trade his way out of these financial problems. Please keep in mind we are not the only ones who have money invested with him. Eighteen million worth to be exact, we have to be patient, just like the others are. Everyone else is very happy and supportive and willing to wait a further twelve months so he can trade out of this disaster. What a kind and considerate man? He wanted us to know that he personally didn't have any financial problems, as he doesn't mix personal with business matters. Unfortunately, our money was invested with a company that has done the wrong thing, however he was the one that chose the company and was investing our clients' funds without our consent. He has appointed lawyers who are dealing with the situation as best *as they can. I had a delightful time with this crazy, lying, cheating scoundrel.*

DAY 11 - Departing Toronto in the morning and jetted off to Edmonton. Another gentleman on our target list. We turned up at his office and gave him the shock of his life. He couldn't believe his eyes, that Ralph had actually just turned up in his office. He unfortunately had appointments and we should have let him know as he wasn't available. Ralph just ignored that and sat down, refusing to leave. The meeting of course went nowhere, he takes no responsibility for the lost funds. Very similar excuses to the one in Toronto, the funds were not invested for long enough which meant they could not trade with them long enough to receive a return. He was very busy, as we could see from all the paperwork on his desk, working through all the investor funds. Give him time and patience and we will see a return on investment. Thank you for coming all this way, I shall be in touch shortly with some good news. Rubbish.

After that waste of time, we jumped on a flight to Vancouver. Here we spent time with a friend. We were able to sleep on his boat for two nights, it was lovely being rocked to sleep by the gentle swaying of the sea.

DAY 12 - Spent the morning brain storming with our friend trying to figure out the best plan of action. The afternoon was spent at Granville Island, shopping and eating.

DAY 13 - *During the night we were fumigated by petrol fumes from the boat, the tanks had been filled up just before bedtime. It was ghastly and at 5.45am the carbon monoxide alarm sounded, rousing us from our smelly sleep. Great start to the day. We were scheduled to go out on the boat all day, hence why the tanks were filled, but our friend had had a big night out on the town and was in no fit state to take us anywhere. Instead, we enjoyed the day sightseeing and shopping. We then flew to Los Angeles.*

DAY 14 - *Early start. Breakfast with (alias), Sam Spade, our very own private investigator - because everyone needs their own PI. We had a very interesting conversation with Sam, there are many varied and crafty means of recovering lost funds. He has done many successful recoveries and they don't use violence, isn't that good, just very persuasive methods. Once they used needles with saline but pretended it was much more sinister than saline. The bad guy surrendered. Great stuff, the type of recovery I would most certainly use (!?). Sam was adamant that this was a much better alternative than years going through the court system. Let's go grab them now and use force. Not sure God would approve of this method, very much an eye for an eye. We spent three hours discussing options. After such talk I was more than ready for some retail therapy.*

DAY 15 - *Another meeting with alias, Sam Spade, to explain his costs. Phase one: US$10,000 which is collecting background information. Finding out* *where the players lived, their bank balance and tax file numbers. Phase two: US$10,000, low key surveillance, watching their habits and family. Where do they go and why. Real spy stuff. Phase three: the big one, US$25,000. Here they actually grab them and put them in a room and scare them to death, or until they return the funds. They are not released until the funds are in our account.*

Can you believe this stuff? And Ralph is actually considering it. Sam explains that our identities are not revealed to the snatched as it could put our lives in danger in the future. That's very comforting. I am sure I am currently living my life on a movie set. What happened to the quiet suburban life? Sam has one more thing - once the funds are recovered, he then receives twenty percent of the funds.

We leave the meeting with our heads spinning. We spend the afternoon at factory outlets shopping for bribes to take back to the girls. Tonight, we travel home, back to my normal busy life. Bring it on.

Our overseas escapade was futile in the end; Ralph did file a suit with the local authorities and an investigation was done however it is hard to return money when the money cannot be found. Years later, a very small portion of the stolen funds was returned.

Chapter 7

OUR PROPERTY

DURING MY THIRTIETH year, after I had returned from my two weeks of marriage separation, our home renovations were nearly complete. Ralph was convinced we were going to be billionaires and he was retiring at forty. Deciding we needed to sell our home, the place where we were to start a home church, he instead bought a five-acre property. I have to say, I completely freaked out. How on earth could we afford to do that? But I was not allowed to question him. He believed God told him to buy this property and I had to have the faith to believe this. He managed to negotiate a great price, five percent deposit and a six-month settlement. It would seem God was most definitely opening the door. Was this Victory or

Sinister at work? It would seem Victory, as I was about to own a horse property and after 15 years of no horse, I would have the opportunity to enjoy my passion for horses once again, along with my daughters. I truly loved living on acres and having horses, but there is always a cost, and Sinister used many occasions to bring me down.

We had six months to finish the renovations, pack up the house and then sell. All this while I was working at Little Munchkins. It was stressful! Three months before moving, it was Christmas, and we decided to buy the girls ponies, and found somewhere to stable them while waiting to move. I also found the perfect horse for me, Waffles. He became my rock through the many rocky years ahead. Now that we had added horses to our day, life was busy.

We sold our current home without any difficulty, except it still was not quite finished upon settlement day and Ralph was still racing around getting it done. Even after we moved out and the new owners moved in, Ralph was renovating the downstairs area. I have to say he had done an amazing job with the renovations, it looked great, and considering he wasn't a builder he did an exceptional job. The stress he placed upon himself, though, was next level, so we all struggled with our emotions. Our lives were always running at warp speed and very close to the edge of collapsing. Even the finance for the property was touch and go and came through at the very last moment. Now remember we are not dealing with the average husband - we have to understand that nothing is straight forward, ever. We couldn't just get a mortgage and pay it off like everyone else. One of the companies Ralph had set up, purchased the property, and then leased it back to us. I assume the reason behind this was for tax purposes. It went against everything Ralph stood for - tax paying that is!

The day we moved to our horse property we had the entire extended family over and we explained to the children that there could possibly be snakes, so wear shoes, and do not run if you come across one. Lo and behold a red belly black snake appeared on the path to the stables, we had children screaming and running in all directions. Great start. Snakes never worried me, but spiders are a totally different story. When you live on the edge of the Australian bush you must learn to contend with lots of creepy crawlies.

Let me take a moment to describe our new home. It was situated at the bottom of a big hill on five acres, cut off from everything but still in suburbia. There were only four other properties on our road. The house was two storeys with a granny flat attached. It was a poorly designed house as the kitchen and lounge room really needed to face the back of the property so you could see all the action, but instead they faced the front garden - which was lovely, but the children, pool and horses were out the back. But the beauty of this place wasn't about the house itself but about the property, this was where the magic was. There was a pool with a spa, a tennis court, nine stables with yards so the horses were not just locked in a small box at night, and a small dam with an island for the ducks to be secure at night. There was also a creek that ran through the middle of the property, but due to a drought there wasn't a lot of water running through it. The paddocks were all grassed, and I loved that they were large, so the horses had plenty of grass and plenty of room. I wanted the horses to have the best facilities possible, which is tricky on a small acreage. We also had an arena with mirrors and a round yard for the horses. I was truly blessed to own such a magnificent property.

This property was designed for horse agistment and on purchasing it we had inherited several horses and their owners. Having a horse agistment property meant you were constantly sharing your space with others. There were always people around, so if you were into having your own space to yourself, then this was not the lifestyle for you. I made many new friends while living here. That's not to say we all got on famously - there were times when people and horses became a challenge. We had one lady who constantly cleaned her horse's yard with just her bra on, no shirt - this was not really appropriate! Another girl had a highly strung horse that never stopped running, which was not good for the paddock as it turned it to dirt. Horse people can be extremely demanding but the people who kept their horses at our place were lovely, we all managed to get along really well. We often had extra visitors in the form of diamond pythons, they loved to curl up on the hay in the feed shed as it was warm. These snakes weren't dangerous to humans, and I learnt to boldly pick them up and relocate them, so others did not freak out. They were handy to have as they kept the mice and rats away. I just hoped they did not take a liking to one of our cats.

The first couple of years Ralph helped with the running of things, he would spend two hours every morning cleaning out the stables and then weekends maintaining everything. He enjoyed it as it was very different to office work - but it wasn't long before he lost interest. There was a world out there that needed him, and he had much more interesting things to do. That of course meant I had the responsibility now of looking after everything at home. Ralph had started travelling extensively and it was my responsibility to look after the property and horses while he was away, and to the highest standard.

A typical day: I would wake up at 6am, go feed the horses breakfast and change their rugs, come wake up the girls, organise their breakfast and lunches. I would then run outside and put the horses in the paddocks, clean out the stables, back inside for shower, drive the girls to school, then arrive to Little Munchkins by 8.30am. I'd work all day with parents and children, the girls would catch the bus to Munchkins, they would have a play and then do their homework. When we arrived home, we would all go bring the horses in, feed them, put their night rugs on and make up the feeds for the following day. I was very blessed to have daughters who helped, although at times Harmony protested. I could not have done it without their cooperation. We all had to be very organised and keep to a schedule. Unfortunately, one morning in our haste to get to school, Melody had forgotten to change from slippers to shoes, and it wasn't until we arrived at school that she realised. This caused all sorts of heartache as she was not about to wear slippers all day and she felt terrible for not realising. The car had become like a wardrobe on wheels and thankfully we found a pair of sneakers. Melody was not happy about breaking school rules, but it was better than slippers! For three years I did this routine, it was insane, and when I look back on it, I have no idea how I did it. There was no time for any of us girls to get sick, there was no time for a day off, it was nonstop action. We also had our own horses which needed to be ridden, which we could only do on weekends. One thing was for sure, Ralph could not accuse me of being lazy. It was definitely supernatural strength that got me through.

Ralph had a habit of fixating on things, one of which was Y2K. He was convinced that there was going to be a catastrophic event on January 1, 2000. This was the major reason he was selling our other home, with renovations barely completed, and buying five acres. Once we moved in, we apparently had six months before the end of the world as we knew it and there was much to be done. The property had to be set up to be a place for people to come and stay safe, yes, just like a typical end-of-days movie. Ralph purchased non-perishable food, petrol and endless loads of toilet paper and sanitary pads. This event consumed him, and I am convinced that the money being used to purchase this property and storing up the necessities was not money he had actually earned. What would that matter - when the world collapsed no one was going to worry about their investments, as the world economy would no longer exist! We had everything set up and ready, and on New Year's Eve walked up to the top of our hill just before midnight where we could see the city in the distance - we were ready for the lights to go out. We had tins of sardines; we were safe! I'm laughing, because of course the lights stayed on. Great. We were now going to have to live on tinned food forever while the rest of society enjoyed fresh fruit and vegetables. Oh well, at least we would not have to buy petrol for a while, we had massive drums of it.

After this debacle, which I was not allowed to make a big deal about, Ralph then went on a quest to turn our property into a sovereign State. He studied Hutt River, which is a place in Western Australia that had become a sovereign State many years ago. Yes, this is what was next on our agenda. He was going to purchase the other properties on our road, put a boom gate at the top of the hill and be the prince of his own territory. You must understand how good he was at convincing people that whatever he spoke was truth, and when things did not go according to Ralph, no one was brave enough to point out that he was wrong. It was impossible to buy all the properties, and of course the sovereign State was never going to happen, so the idea eventually faded into the background.

When you purchase a property in New South Wales you have to pay stamp duty on the day of settlement. Ralph thought that he was not expected to pay this. He did not pay taxes of any kind, the Government made enough money from road, petrol and other taxes. How were we going to settle without paying? Easy, you write a company cheque, finalise the purchase and then cancel the cheque. This actually worked, and he was so proud of himself. It was six years later when the Commissioner of State Revenue finally caught up to him and he was asked to pay the amount due plus interest. There was no way he was paying that, so off he went to court. He offered them $45,000 plus legal fees as that was all he could afford, so they could accept that or spend years in court. They accepted it, even though it was less than the actual stamp duty owed.

On another occasion, the taxation department tried to take him on for unpaid taxes. Off he went to court again, his argument was he was not a qualified tax accountant, which meant he couldn't sign the tax pack. He was unable to put his signature on this legal document as he may have inadvertently made a mistake, and by signing the form he was then liable. He was more than happy to complete the forms, but refused to sign them, which made them invalid. He assured the courts that his companies were above reproach, and he paid the relevant taxes when required, but as his companies were non-profit, tax was a very small amount. Again, he was happy to spend years in court arguing about this. He had the courts scratching their heads, struggling to refute what he had said, and they let him off. This just fed his ego and gave him an enormous amount of power. Nothing could stand in his way, not even the law of the land. He obviously had a legitimate argument, he believed, otherwise they would have pursued this further. I can honestly say I did not understand any of it, it was way beyond my comprehension.

Little Munchkins closed its doors in 2002 and Sinister by then was in full swing, with things starting to go from bad to worse rapidly. I no longer had a business that was open seven days a week, so I was back to being labelled lazy. Ralph travelled extensively throughout this year, he would be gone for six to eight weeks at a time, and back for maybe two weeks in between. He always planned his return around my monthly cycle as it was very important to him that I was available to satisfy his needs. He was a man who was out in the world doing God's work and when home his wife was expected to be available. This is very hard to do physically when you are being emotionally assaulted. He would treat me with total disrespect, but still expected me to willingly 'turn it on' whenever he wanted. I never felt loved, cherished, or appreciated. I realise the importance of intimacy in a relationship, and I was a disappointment to him. I regret this, and I wish I could have gladly, enthusiastically given to him what he needed. I was never confident around him, I was never good enough at anything, so I believed the same about me when it came to satisfying my husband. I wish I had addressed this issue, but I have learnt over the years that unless you are feeling loved and appreciated as a woman, it is very hard to satisfy your husband in the bedroom.

When Ralph came back from one of his trips, he would arrive home and criticise everyone about everything. We had a lovely Christian girl that helped maintain the property and the horses with me, but Ralph was so critical of her work that she was traumatised and had to leave for her own sanity. We employed another young woman to take her place, she was a lot more resilient but still found working for him near impossible. He was never satisfied with anything any of us did, even though he was not around to assist in any way.

We all dreaded Ralph's return home. He drank an excessive amount of tea, or so we thought; I believe it was actually scotch. We were not allowed to disturb him in his important work, which seemed to go on 24 hours a day. He wasn't actually working a lot of these hours; he was often on social media and chatting on the phone to those he liked. We were not his favourite people as we did not benefit him in any way, which meant we were not a priority.

For years Ralph never came to dinner on time so I tried to get tricky and would say dinner was ready ten minutes before it was, but he was still always late. We would have to wait for him to arrive at the table before we were allowed to start. It was all these subtle undermining happenings that kept the girls and I on edge. The girls craved his attention when he was home and would beg him to play with them on the trampoline. His stock standard answer was "in a minute, I'll be there in a minute." Great, off they would go, bouncing on the trampoline waiting patiently for their dad. They would wait hours for him to turn up, when they eventually got tired of waiting, they would go and ask him again. His cutting response was "you want to live here on this property, I have to work to pay for it." It would break my heart as these girls didn't care where they lived, they just wanted their dad to spend time with them.

On another occasion just before he arrived home, I organised a skip bin to clean up the property, as I didn't want him to complain about the mess. We worked really hard, and the place looked amazing. He screamed at me for wasting money on a skip bin when the tip was just up the road. He was furious. It didn't matter what we did or how hard we tried to please him; we could never get it right. There were many incidents where he would blow up at us, so we lived in fear of his return, and we wrote the day of his return on the calendar as D Day. I was a fun-loving person who loved life and people, but when the day was approaching, I would become moody and panicked.

In hindsight I believe he was drinking a lot more than I realised and most likely already attending sex clubs when he travelled. I found out later from his credit card statement that he was going to these clubs. He no doubt was struggling to maintain control of both his worlds. He was becoming consumed with money, sex, and power.

I did not know how much longer I could continue.

This was not a life I wanted for myself or the girls, but I struggled with the idea of divorce as I still believed marriage was for life. It was impossible to communicate with him, his belief was we should just submit to him, he was the head of the household.

The time came when Ralph eventually asked us to move to Estonia, as he was tired of all the travelling and Estonia was where his calling was. I believed this was our only option if I wanted to stay married, so I approached the school about educating the girls via correspondence. The school was very open to the idea if we kept paying the school fees. The girls and I started preparing ourselves for a massive upheaval. Ralph kept delaying us coming, giving excuses about not being ready for us to be there as certain things needed to be set up first. He was full of promises and ideas and planned on building a massive log cabin with an indoor pool and a basketball court. He was all talk, there was no money. I started to prepare myself by thinking of ways I could keep myself busy over there so I would not be accused of being lazy. I came up with the brilliant idea of opening a fish and chip shop as there was no such thing in Estonia. I was shot down though, I was told I should be content to just come and live there to be with him, why would I have to find things to do? Sigh. He truly believed he was called to ministry over there and he was going to be heavily involved with the local church and getting teens off the streets. Nothing like this ever happened.

I believe the motivation for us going to live in Estonia was all about selling our property, which had dramatically increased in value, and utilising this money to fund his latest projects. These included a bit of church charity work, but more accurately, it was all about building his personal empire. I did not want to sell the property as I knew once it was gone there would be no coming back to my city. I wanted to rent it out and make sure that we were called to live in Estonia. But he was very adamant that I was to submit to his authority which God had placed on him as my husband. I told him I would pray about it, but I was quickly told that there was no need as he had direct communication with God as the head of the house, and my job was to submit.

Chapter 8

ALL CREATURES GREAT & SMALL

THE GIRLS AND I loved this home, and over time we added many animals to our household. Jupiter the springer spaniel, Peggy the Airedale, Faith the toy poodle, our cats Kinky, Alaska and Clogs, ducks Splish and Splash, guinea fowl to keep the snakes away, rabbits, and our horses. After I had closed Little Munchkins, I started to become more involved with the horses and the property, and start breeding Haflingers, Austrian mountain horses. At one stage we had Waffles, my riding horse, Ladybird, his sister whom Melody rode, as well as Maya and Lisha, mares that we bred with. Harmony had her pony, Tex, who was a great horse. Animals are placed in our lives for sheer entertainment. We are blessed to have them in our lives. Victory often uses animals to give us joy, which our animals certainly did.

Before I regale you with stories about these animals, let me begin with some tales of a couple of animals we had before the property. Ralph and I started our married life in a garden flat with a Burmese cat, Snuggles. She was the fur baby we all have before children arrive. In other words, very spoilt. We taught her to jump into our arms when we clapped and to sit around our neck. We once had a visitor clap his hands, and the next minute Snuggles jumped up onto his chest expecting arms around her, but alas she just slid down his body to the floor. The poor man had no idea what just happened. Snuggles was a great first pet. Once we moved into our own home we could add to the cat with a dog. Our first dog was an Old English sheep dog, she was lovely, but one day our pastor and family came over for lunch and she bit their daughter, not hard, but the child was pulling on her fur, and she reacted. The pastor never came back for a meal again. After she passed away, we decided on a Newfoundland, Brittany. She weighed around 50 kilos, a lovely dog, but she had the habit of helping herself to the washing on the line - but only garments that were red! There was one terrible incident where she had wandered up the road and came back with a fully roasted leg of lamb. I had no idea where it came from but imagine the family when they went to sit down for dinner and the roast had disappeared. I do wonder what they would have thought.

When the girls were little, we bought them a toy poodle, Bundles, and they adored her. While we were away and we had a friend look after the house and animals, she went missing. The girls were devastated. A few months later, we saw her at the shops with another family, and we told them that was our dog, but they denied it - and as we had no way of proving it was Bundles as pets were not microchipped then, we had to leave her with them. I still remember the tears the girls cried; they could not understand why they would not give our dog back.

Now for the animals that were a part of life on the property. If there was a chair not pushed in, Jupiter the springer spaniel would climb onto the table and help himself to any food that was available. We as a family knew this so we always made sure the dogs were outside. However, our friends did not know this - so Jupiter would wait for a visitor to arrive and follow them into the house. One friend put a lovely, iced bun on the table once and then came outside to find us. Jupiter was not well after she devoured it. As for Peggy, she was the most mischievous dog there was. Every morning she would go down to the dam to see if the ducks had laid eggs, and if there was one, she would carry it back to the house and place it on the front door mat. This worked well for years until one day she dropped it and found out what was inside the shell. We never received door-to-door delivery after that! Peggy loved to help us put the horses in their designated paddocks every morning. We did not have to lead the horses as they knew which paddock was their paddock, so Peggy just helped them get there a bit quicker. One year she had eleven puppies, thanks to the German Shepherd up the road, and when they were old enough to follow mum around, they would help put the horses out. It was so cute to see Peggy with a trail of puppies, making sure the work was done. We had friends who lived in the country, and they once gave us a lamb whose mother had rejected her. Peggy adopted her, and we called her Mary because Peggy had a little lamb, Mary. Made sense to us! This lamb believed she was a dog, she had her own dog bed, and expected dog biscuits when they all got fed. Mary also came to do the horses, but instead of putting them in the paddocks she would jump up on all the bales of hay. Being territorial, Peggy would chase cars that came down our road: not the cars that belonged to any of our neighbours, only cars that did not belong. Mary soon learnt the joy of chasing cars, too. The two of them would go bounding up the road chasing unknown cars back up the hill. Now Mary really was a sheep, and as such not only enjoyed dog biscuits but also plants. She once took a liking to our Birds of Paradise; down both sides of the stem were teeth marks. We had a very nice display of these plants but now they looked munched on. Ralph returned from one of his trips and lost the plot, his prized plants had been destroyed. It wasn't long after that, Mary was delivered back to the farm. We missed her, she was so entertaining and full of life. As for the Birds of Paradise, the following year they came out in total splendour, they were more brilliant in their display than ever before. They just needed a good prune from a delightful little lamb.

The girls wanted as many animals as I allowed, and why not? We had the space. There was even a time we had seahorses! Fascinating to watch but very hard to look after. Should have stuck with sea monkeys! Faith, our new toy poodle, once got in the way of one of the ponies and was kicked, she had to have a hip operation, but she recovered and learnt to never go near the horses. We lost a lot of our pets to ticks, for such a tiny pest they sure are deadly.

I once decided to buy Ralph a Bassett hound for his birthday, but I did not want a puppy, so I found an adult one, Ringo. Ralph had always wanted a Bassett hound, and I thought it would be the perfect gift. I was so wrong; Ralph came home and was very happy with his gift but unfortunately Ringo hated him. He never stopped barking when Ralph was around. It did not go down very well, everyone and everything was supposed to love Ralph. Ringo did not stay long in our family.

The girls and I started to get very involved in natural horsemanship, and the main reason for this was because my horse, Waffles was such a handful. Natural horsemanship helped us to understand the horse from the ground up. Harmony and I (unfortunately Melody was too young) attended some horsemanship camps, they were great fun, and we even had a few clinics at our place. We had the perfect set up for them. There was one camp that I attended with Waffles, and he was being a gentleman for the most part. However, his patience had limits. If I asked him to move around me in a circle, not a problem - so long as it was only seven times. Anymore and he just left. Now this horse was a Haflinger and as such was very strong. The instructor wanted to show me and everyone else at the clinic how to make Waffles stay the course and do as many circles as necessary. The thing is, Waffles thought that if he did the circles well, why overdo it? The instructor had no problems, Waffles was behaving and looking good, and then came the eighth circle and he knew exactly what he was planning to do. As soon as the instructor relaxed and started saying how good he was, Waffles took off. The instructor tried holding on to the rope for dear life - not a good idea - and consequently ended with bad rope burn. Waffles knew he had blown it big time, so he did the only thing he could, he dived into the massive dam that was on this property and stood in the middle of it so no one could reach him. This horse made me laugh!

The instructor told us it was time for lunch. After lunch he returned all bandaged up and informed me that this horse was no good and that I needed a new one. Of course, I didn't listen, he was full of character, that was all, and you should never have asked for that eighth circle. He was cheeky and naughty, but he was mine and he carried me through some of my toughest years that were still ahead. Victory placed him in my life at the right time and for the right reasons. I was accused of loving him more than my husband, but as you have already read, that was understandable. Waffles did not like to be contained. If a fence wasn't electrified, he just leant on it until it fell over or jumped over the gate. We had to electrify all the fences, and the horses knew it, but many of the girls' friends were not aware, and many a friend received a zap.

Harmony's first horse was Victoria, a nasty mare as it turned out, who bit and kicked and bucked. She didn't last long; she was too much for Harmony. Next, Harmony and I found Tex, from Nimbin, he was a palomino with a heart of gold. He was a delightful horse, so accommodating, anyone could ride him. We always said jokingly that he was mellow because he was bought up on the Nimbin special weed.

Harmony was a good rider, but I do remember one incident where we were hosting a clinic, and we had to shut our eyes and trust our horse to walk around the arena. Tex was a legend but Harmony with her eyes closed became unbalanced and ended up slipping to the side. Very uncomfortable for the horse but Tex did not mind. I have known a lot of horses and I would have to say this horse was the best children's pony a parent could ask for.

Melody's first horse was Sally, and she came with a bonus, her foal, Phoenix. They were Shetlands. Shetlands are not so well behaved, they do bite, and they are stubborn, nevertheless Melody loved her and rode her until she outgrew her. Melody then decided she had a love for Haflingers just like her mum. We purchased Ladybird, Waffles' sister who was hard work. Typical mare, she was highly strung, jumpy and a very nervous horse. It was terrifying watching Melody ride her because you just did not know how long she would have the privilege before ending up out of the saddle and on the ground. Even just mounting her was a challenge, if you flapped the stirrup she would buck, if you even blew your nose while riding, she would buck. Melody spent a lot of time on the ground, but it never stopped her from riding her beloved Ladybird, and she was never seriously injured. I am sure Victory had something to do with that. As Melody got older and stronger Ladybird became more confident and the two of them had a great relationship, although you could never trust her one hundred percent.

We also had two Haflinger breeding mares, Alisha and Maya. Unfortunately, we didn't keep Maya for long as we couldn't afford to, and my world was starting to crack. Lisha came to us with a foal, Atomic, and she had another which we named, Little Miss. We also had Ladybird put in foal and she delivered us Africa. The foals were adorable, and we had a huge amount of fun with them. When Little Miss was being born, Melody was in the thick of it. In the middle of the night, she was there assisting Lisha, and helped pull Little Miss free. Melody then assisted with her first feed off her mother. Meanwhile Harmony was also there but throwing up in the corner from seeing all the blood and goop. We missed the birth of our foal Africa, as Ladybird surprised us all by delivering him in the paddock while the girls were at school, and I was off at work. Ladybird was in the paddock with Waffles, and he decided the foal was his and would not let Ladybird near him. My horse, I tell you he never made it easy. We had to separate them for a time.

When Little Miss was a few days old she collapsed and was paralysed. We found a shellback tick on her. Usually, these nasty deadly ticks had no effect on horses, but because she was a newborn it had paralysed her. The vet had no idea what to do so we had to load her and Lisha onto a horse float and take her to Randwick horse hospital. They had to treat her with the serum that they use for dogs and hope it would work, which it did. After ten days in hospital, she was allowed home. The incident was written up in several vet journals so other vets would know what to do if it ever happened again.

Our horses gave us so much pleasure. Yes, they were time consuming, and we had extremely busy lives, but they kept us sane. The girls had friends over all the time, and I did not give it much thought, but the girls were far more educated in the animal kingdom than their friends. It was Melody who not only enjoyed riding but also the everyday horse owning life. One time she had a friend over so they could watch the castration of Atomic. Chop off came his bits - Melody was impressed, not so much the friend. Another friend was horrified when she witnessed the size of a horse penis, a rather large appendage, and then saw the house mount one of the mares. It is quite confronting watching horses do their thing, it is messy, loud, and brutal. I had to ring the girls' mother and apologise. One of the horses that belonged to a boarder we had staying with us, ripped her shoulder in a big L shape, and the cut went down to the bone. The vet was called, and Melody just stood watching in fascination has the horse was sedated and repaired. Luckily that day there were no friends visiting. Melody's fascination with the vet's work that day, would blossom later in life into her own pursuit of a veterinary career. We had many others boarding their horses with us over the years and many became lifelong friends. There is a unique and exquisite bond between a rider and their horse, but it was also a community of like-minded people that bonded over all things horse. Melody was the farm girl and Harmony the city girl.

Ralph, yes, he must be mentioned. He tried riding Waffles once. This did not end well. He was in the arena and Waffles just turned around, took off and jumped over the pole that covered the entrance. Ralph fell off but was not injured. He never tried riding another horse of ours again. There was one time when he was showing off the horses to a couple of his friends. One of them wanted to ride Waffles. He was a magnificent looking horse with his caramel coat, and thick white mane and tail, so everybody wanted to ride him. Ralph insisted I let her ride, and who was I to argue. The woman jumped on and began riding and Waffles looked like butter wouldn't melt in his mouth - but he thought about his options for trouble making and came up with the idea of lying down. He just stopped and lay down on the ground. Smart horse.

The girls would often have friends over and of course they all wanted pony rides. Ladybird was not an option so we would saddle up Tex and Waffles. You see, Waffles was amazing with children, he never did anything to harm them, he was happy to let them crawl all over him, kick him unnecessarily and even stand on him. He loved children.

At one point we had to relocate our horses to other properties, and they became very well known within the community. The problem with Waffles was he did not like to be contained and the grass was always greener on the other side. He would just lean on a fence until it gave way and then jump out and take the others with him. They would find themselves another place to eat grass. Many a time I had to go catch them and return them to their paddock. Everyone knew of these naughty Haflingers. There were a few unhappy property owners who did not appreciate horses munching on the manicured lawns.

So, what happened to all our horses? Ralph at one stage tried to repossess them. He told me that they were owned by the company that had leased the property to us, the one that he was a director of, such rubbish. I informed him that the horses were given to us as presents, for Christmas or for birthdays, they were not owned by a company. He relented. The mares and the foals had to be sold as I could not afford to keep them. We kept our riding ponies. Tex had to be put down just after Harmony finished her High School Certificate as he had cancer. We could not afford the extensive treatment and there was no guarantee it would work. I did not want to see him suffer so I had to make the hardest decision. It was an awful day with lots of tears, we were devastated that his life was cut short. As for Waffles and Ladybird I eventually had to find them a new home, which no horse lover wants to do. I found a place a few hours away called Hope Hill which helped children in crisis from low socio-economic areas. Children would spend a few days with the horses learning about horsemanship and enjoying their company. They had lots of grass and lots of space and we were allowed to visit them whenever we wanted.

After having Waffles for fourteen years, it was a hard decision to let him go but Melody had moved to Melbourne to study, and it was very expensive owning horses. The two horses were a pair, and I could not separate them, so when this opportunity came up for them to be in ministry and together, I had to let them go. I miss him every day. There is always that one special horse that saved you from yourself, and Waffles was that for me. The Hope Hill property was sold a couple of years ago and I was given the opportunity to have the two horses back, but it is way too expensive to own a horse where I live, on a travel agent's wage. They have now found a home with Riding for the Disabled and are still helping children. I do miss my horse as he played such an important part in the healing of my heart, but he is doing the Lord's work. Victory reigns.

Chapter 9

END OF A MARRIAGE

AFTER SIXTEEN YEARS of marriage and trying so desperately to make it work, I was running out of energy. Ralph came home for his 40th birthday and it wasn't long before he went into one of his rages because his precious ride-on lawnmower had been left out in the rain. In all the haste to get the property up to scratch we had forgotten to put it away. I broke, I told him it was over, and I couldn't keep going. He hated everything about me so why on earth would he want to be with me. I was messed up, for years I had shut my emotions down but when I finally gave up and went wild. I screamed and cried and nearly took a gate off its hinges. My parents were at the time staying in our granny flat. I went in there in such a state, my dad thought Ralph had hit me. He went storming off to confront him, Ralph assured him that he would never hit a woman. He did, just not physically. Verbal and emotional abuse over years is far more damaging. Ralph had organised his 40th with some friends so we still had to go through with the party. It was strained and such a horrible situation to participate in when you are going through such pain and turmoil. I was mentally spent. I remember doing the horses the following morning and Melody came and asked if I was okay, and I broke down in tears. I told her that I could not stay married any longer and I was so sorry that I couldn't. She hugged me tight and told me it was all going to be okay. When Ralph found out I had told her he was livid. I really wasn't functioning well and had no idea of separation protocol.

Ralph left the country the following day. My dad came to speak to me, and we discussed how hard this was going to be. Ralph did not fail at anything and to have a failed marriage, no matter how dysfunctional, was not acceptable. Ralph was going to get nasty, and that was an understatement. Dad wanted to make sure I was prepared for a battle, but I had no idea this battle would be raging for the remainder of my current life. This year of separation was a nightmare. A roller coaster ride of emotions and hurts where Sinister came to destroy and pull down all that he could. However, there were precious moments where Victory sprinkled me with the power of God's love.

I am going to share my diary entries for the following twelve months as they mark the moments and events in real time.

09 May, 2003

I wonder if I would have been happier if he worked a normal job and we lived a normal suburban life. Ralph says he would have been miserable, there is no way he would settle for mediocre when there was a world to conquer. I wonder whether losing his family and many of his friends has been worth it. I know his attitude is "I'll show them, I'll prove I can make a billion dollars". He states that I have a very low self-esteem, but I think maybe he does, as he is the one always trying to do better than everyone else. People say if only you could wind back the clock to happier times, but I don't think he would have stayed happy just living life. It would seem he is really happy now being the international traveller, eating and drinking out several times a week. Being treated like a king by the people he has chosen to surround himself with. I am sure if he had unlimited financial resources, he would be a different man, kinder. Despite having money or not it still boils down to attitude. My life is falling apart all around me but I can still treat people with love, respect and kindness. Ralph is cruel to all those who stand against him.

16 May, 2003

The tears are still falling, they never stop. I'm convinced that God has several water tanks of my tears stored up in heaven. I received an email from Ralph today explaining he had a bad attitude towards our church movement, the AOG (Assemblies of God) and he has asked them to forgive him. This is a first, you must remember Ralph does not believe he has ever done anything wrong. Wow, is he seeing the light?

I feel the need to write about a woman named Katie, so I need to digress for a moment to explain. Katie is the daughter of Ralph's best friend, and she decided to go to Estonia and work for Ralph. I did not see anything wrong with this at the time, but in 2002, Ralph requested that the girls and I go visit him in Estonia. The three of us flew out at the beginning of July and had a week in Hawaii and a few days in San Francisco on the way. We had a great time, except for one major issue. We were in Hawaii for Melody's birthday and had a great day out snorkelling off a catamaran, swimming with turtles. Melody could not wait to get a telephone call from her dad so she could tell him all about it. The call never came. He had forgotten her birthday. She was distraught, and it broke my heart. When we landed in Estonia, Ralph was late picking us up (I also remember this happening to me once before in the early years of our marriage), and when he finally showed he was all flustered explaining that he had things to sort out with Katie. He then presented Melody with a book for her birthday that was appropriate for a four-year-old, not a nine-year-old. He then declared he had forgotten her birthday because he was busy with Katie. No apology. Alarm bells start sounding. Why is Katie so important? What is going on? We arrived at his apartment to discover that Katie lived there as well. I had no idea.

Estonia was not a very exciting place for us, with very little English spoken, but we were there to see how we could make it work 'if and when' we moved over. Melody found plenty of cats outside, which she fed regularly while we were there. The morning after our arrival Ralph wanted to take us out for breakfast, and he asked me if I would like pancakes or eggs. I chose pancakes. Katie chose eggs. Katie won.

We went to church on the Sunday and that also was a strange encounter. The preacher was from Australia, in fact this was the person who had told Ralph about Estonia and the Christian work that needed to be done there. I believe he wanted Ralph's financial support more than his Christian assistance. He preached in English, which was handy for us, and had an interpreter, and at the end of his sermon he told us he had a word from God for us. He saw the girls and I working closely with the youth and street kids of Estonia, and we would have a powerful ministry, he then added we would be doing it with Katie. My spirit rebelled. There was no way Katie, and I would be in ministry together as it had become obvious to me that something was going on between her and my husband. After church we went to a restaurant with the local pastors and leaders, for a buffet lunch. The girls and I were asked to help ourselves but Ralph ran around after Katie, getting her food and drinks, whatever she needed. The local pastor kept telling me how much Ralph loved me, and I found that odd. Why the need to constantly tell me? Did he need to be convinced? Things were not right.

I needed to get out of Estonia. When we left Ralph came with us and we travelled to Rome. He had made reservations in an incredibly expensive hotel, which was lovely, but in hindsight he was trying to buy me off, as he had things to hide and guilt to cover up. Rome was a disaster. He was constantly on the phone to Katie and racing around from bank to bank. He had to place money into an investment, or he would miss out. Stop complaining, he said, as this is how he could afford to send us on holidays. The girls and I were on edge the entire time and really could not enjoy ourselves. We had three nights in Rome before arriving in Hong Kong. While in Hong Kong Ralph met with some other investors, and he was becoming decidedly more agitated. After two nights the girls and I left for home and Ralph decided to stay in Hong Kong to get some work done. In hindsight I believe now he was staying to relieve tensions at clubs.

Anyway, back to Ralph asking for forgiveness from the AOG church. He also told me in his email that he had asked Katie to move out of his apartment. Two days later he fired her. I cannot really tell you what happened here except they parted on very bad terms and whatever went down was never discussed with me. I looked at the positive and thought God was moving on his heart and he was making positive changes. How wrong was I? The diary entry continues:

Ralph has forwarded me an email from a pastor friend of his, in which the pastor accuses me of not letting my husband do his Godly work. By separating from Ralph, I am either trying to force him to come home and tear him away from God's work or aiming to get a divorce so I can remarry. He also accused me of passing divorce down to my children. A horrible email from a pastor who has never met me. I do not know what Ralph has told him, but I never had a problem with Ralph living overseas - the problem is when he comes home, he is impossible to please and to live with. He still believes that I am the problem, and he has admitted no guilt.

Is Ralph using God as an excuse? He is called by God, so it is okay to live away from his family. He is called by God, so it is okay to have Katie live with him. He is called by God, so it is okay for him to drink, swear and visit "clubs".

He keeps saying we must come over to Estonia or we are out of the will of God. I am so tempted to pack up and go over there and tell him if he is called by God, so is his family. He would be ecstatic for about a week and then he would get bored with us as we would be cramping his hidden lifestyle and he would send us home. You see it is not us unwilling to work all this out, it is him who cannot admit he does not want us. To admit that is to admit he failed at something.

Time for a more positive diary entry. The girls and I have had so many awesome things happen during these dark days that we've decided to label them our 'mini miracles', the moments where Victory has reigned. Over the course of a month, so many amazing things happened in succession. We had a mare, Maya, that we had purchased for breeding, but we needed to sell her and fast. Within one week she had been purchased back from her original owners for the same price that we had purchased her for. This money enabled us to erect two more stables which would allow us to look after two more horses. More income to keep the property running. Next, we received an insurance payout for a generator that had been stolen a few months back. Victory didn't just give me tangible miracles, but emotional ones, too.

02 June, 2003

I have just finished reading David Wilkinson's book "Hallowed Be Thy Names." The chapter I read today was what I needed to hear. The Holy Spirit covered me in HIs peace so I could sleep soundly, and God gave me a word, "you are not condemned, there is no condemnation in Me." Short and precise and just what I needed. Being able to live in the knowledge that Christ paid the price, has taken on a whole new meaning. His love for me is limitless, encouraging and rewarding. He sees my sins and yet forgives me anyway. Wraps His arms around me and helps me to continue on. I do not wish anyone to have to go through immense trials but when we do, the love of Christ is awesome and sustaining.

More mini miracles. The day after Maya was sold, a lady wanted to buy our two foals. Although this was very sad it was necessary, we wanted them to stay together, and they were. I then received a

$2000 refund on an overpayment for something, which allowed the rates to be paid. I rang my church and told them I had a spare room and a granny flat to rent, and five minutes after talking to them they rang me back. Both were taken by fantastic, young, and enthusiastic Christians. All of them willing to help run the property.

Ralph had made it quite clear by this time that if we didn't stay married, I would be bringing financial ruin upon myself. He told me we were broke as he was earning no money. The well had dried up because I refused to be married. This is where "there is no condemnation" became real. I spent days stressing about my role in our money demise, but God has only promised us provision, not ruin.

I decided to send an email to Ralph, and I made sure it was not negative, only spoken from a broken heart to a man that did the damage, whether intentional or not. He replied with, "You have written 99% truth, please forgive me". This was all I wanted, we could work from a place of forgiveness, I thought. Unfortunately, this did not stick, and he just became nastier over time.

This next part is difficult to put into words. I think I must start by saying I was still in a place where I believed we could sort our marriage out and I was very vulnerable. I always believed in the good in people, especially the father of our children. Ralph made a proposition to me where I would sign documents to have our mortgage increased a *further $500,000, making our mortgage $1.5 million. By doing this he guaranteed he would provide for us until the girls left home. Even if I still wanted to proceed with the divorce, he would continue to pay the mortgage and the school fees. This is where I feel really stupid. I believed him. I signed the papers, mind you, he did not really give me much choice, and I feared him and what he was capable of doing. The $500,000 was sent offshore and that was the last I saw of it. It wasn't long before the mortgage and school fees were no longer getting paid.*

09 July, 2003

Mini miracles - The ride-on mower stopped working, it was expected to cost $200 to repair, turns out it was a flat battery and cost $40. We sold another pony.

Ralph has many excellent qualities, he generally is a good man, but it has always been him first and everybody else second. I wonder if he had really put God first, would he really still be in Estonia? If his heart was surrendered to the Lord, I believe he would be here proving to God and his family that we are first. However, the way he treats us and many others is wrong, he is only out to please himself. A humble man would not dictate to his family, he would lovingly care for his family and lead them to do God's will. I believe I love Ralph, but I don't want to lose what God is now doing in and through me. I feel I have been controlled by Ralph for nine years, since we walked away from church, and I put myself under Ralph's authority and not God's. If Ralph was following closely with the Lord, it may have been alright for a season but the past nine years does not show any good fruit.

There have been things God has turned to good. Melody was born, we purchased our property, a Cambodian orphanage was financed, and a legit charity was established, but there has also been much bad fruit, too. Many people were promised things that never came to pass. Money has been mismanaged, money becoming the motivation to break up families. This is not Christian works that Ralph lives in Estonia for - it is for money. The many destroying words Ralph has spoken over his extended family, people in leadership and authority and us, his family, have caused irreparable damage. These key people in his life should be uplifted before God, not downtrodden and condemned. He should be spending time in prayer for those that he believes are against him. Instead, he plots revenge.

Today I surrender my all to Christ. I would give up everything if I thought it was compromising my salvation – but I'm secure in His love. God has blessed me with my wonderful daughters, an amazing property that provides an income, great friends and a loving family. I am now a vibrant member of a positive church. If breaking up my marriage brought me closer to God, then unfortunately it has been worth it. I pray my marriage will be restored but before that can happen Ralph needs to change, as do I. I will no longer let Ralph rule my life, God will. Going *regularly to church is a must. Feeling comfortable with what Ralph does with other people's money is a must. Not feeling condemned for having an opinion is a must.*

In all things I will trust the Lord for He and only He has my best interest at heart.

11 August, 2003

Our first counselling session. I went into shutdown, and we spent most of the meeting talking about Ralph. He believes his love tank has been empty for ten years and mine only five. I cannot remember if there was ever a time where Ralph built me up and didn't belittle me. I was never good at massage- not strong enough. I was never good at sex- not kinky enough. I was not good at talking - put my foot in it too much. He informed the counsellor that I had an inferiority complex but isn't it interesting how I am a confident woman when he is not around. When he is present, I am scared I will say the wrong thing. It is him that has made me feel insecure. He pointed out that my love language was words of affirmation, but he has never once, since we married, told me he loves me.

16 August, 2003

Our next counselling session, what a disaster. If I didn't have the love of God wrapping His strong arms around me, I believe I would have committed suicide. It was a kind of lynching and absolute verbal abuse, and the hardest part was the counsellor didn't stop him. He was quoting scripture about being a submissive wife, he told me I was useless at everything, that I had done nothing well in my life. However, he was still willing to keep his worthless trash as long as I submitted to his authority. I should be grateful that he was still willing to keep me as his wife, but I would need to still receive counselling until he saw a vast improvement. He made it clear that I never fulfilled him, never made him happy and we had no compatibility. If he felt so strongly about this why on earth would he want me as a wife? Surely, he would want a wife that would satisfy him. The issue was he didn't want to tell the world that something in his life failed. He would rather put up with me than get a divorce. He then informed the counsellor that our marriage was easily fixed, I just needed to iron his clothes, live in Estonia and give continuous sex in fifteen different positions. He believes he is perfect and once I accepted my imperfections the marriage will work.

This session was intense, and no words can describe the utter devastation. I walked out after 40 minutes as I just couldn't take any more. I remember driving to collect the girls from a friends' place and I was sobbing and convulsing with spasms racking my body. I wanted to drive into a tree, but I had two precious girls to look after and a God who loved me no matter how useless I felt.

The following day the counsellor rang and apologised for not stopping Ralph in his tirade. He could not believe that a man could be so verbally *abusive towards his wife. He told me to get out, do not stay in the marriage. He had never advised anyone to get a divorce but in my case, I needed to get out as quickly as possible.*

10 October, 2003

It has been three weeks since Ralph left, and I have days with Victory of great joy and faith and other days with Sinister of despair and guilt. My car was repossessed last week as the repayments had not been met. I had no idea it still had money owing as the finances were Ralph's department and I wasn't to interfere. I sent him a text letting him know and his one-word response was, "sad". I was given a scripture from a friend, "God has not given me a spirit of fear but of power, love and a sound mind." Ralph has been in control for a long time, I am not to fear him. He has no regard for my feelings or well-being. He has dictated to me long enough. I am not to doubt that God is with me, He sees my heart and sees my soul. I lived to please my husband and failed miserably, but it wasn't from lack of trying, it wasn't from lack of love, there was just no pleasing him. God has promised me restoration. He will supply my every need. This mere man will not stand in the way of Victory. Everyday my mini miracles astound me. Sometimes it is financial help, sometimes sending the right person along to build up my faith, sometimes to give me peace while I rest. As much as this pains me now, I look forward to the future. I cannot wait to see what God will do. Victory.

November, 2003

Ralph has moved in with someone. He is extremely happy, she has two boys, so now he has the perfect family, two boys and two girls. It is a strange sensation finding out your life partner has found another. It hasn't taken him long to move on but at this stage I don't think I will ever move on. My prayer at this moment is that the girls will be protected from guilt and hurt, that their Heavenly Father will bring them strength and peace, and they will always follow closely after the things of God. We will grow spiritually strong together.

Chapter 10

THE DIARY CONTINUES

A NOTHER YEAR IS upon us. I continue with my diary entries.

01 January, 2004

Throughout last year I have received a constant barrage of abusive emails. I know he sends them to disrupt my life, which is precisely what they do. He sent me one at Christmas - "as of today our mortgage will no longer be paid", unless he finds himself flushed with cash again. Then the mortgage will be paid until such time as the property is sold and then I will owe him for however long it has taken to sell. I am slightly confused; in October he was renting it back to me for free for ten years.

November he was giving me the house and now December I have been thrown out. It totally amazes me how he thinks the girls would want to live with him for several months of the year when he treats us like this. I am forever grateful that Victory has control over my life. My battle is not against flesh and blood and my angels are in a deep and intense war for me. This is a spiritual battle against Sinister, Ralph is not the issue, it is the demons that torment him.

I am unsure where we are going to live, we might have to move to Queensland as it will be more affordable. Who knows, except Victory, what the year will hold. Just keep looking up, follow closely after the Lord and train my girls to do the same. Know that through all my spiritual battles my heart is pure, my heart is good, and my very own angels are waging a war for me. My year goal is to carefully and prayerfully walk us through this year with as little scarring as possible.

2004 hits hard. Ralph has snapped. In 2003 he was still open to looking after us, making sure we had a home and the girls were looked after, but all that changed in 2004. Sinister could see that I was taking back ground, and was not happy. My neighbour and I were discussing him buying our F250 ute before it became repossessed. I was communicating with Ralph about a price, and I believed progress was being made. Then Ralph had someone ring my neighbour's wife and tell her the neighbour was sleeping with me. Ralph also started sending me text messages saying you are a bitch, and you are two faced. He really believed I was sleeping with a married man. It was totally bizarre. The crazy thing was that his wife believed it too and ran off to Queensland. It turns out that Ralph was having me followed by a private investigator and because the neighbour had been over a few times to discuss the purchase of the F250 it must clearly mean an affair was afoot. He had cracked it. This was only the start of years of crazy accusations. Sinister had a hold of him.

January, Continued...

Ralph is also refusing to sign the agency agreement which allows the sale of the property. The bank is ready to take repossession as the mortgage has not been paid for three months. It makes absolutely zero sense to not sign the papers, he just wants to cause maximum trouble. I have also received a fine from ASIC for not putting in company returns because unfortunately I am still the company secretary, even though I have nothing to do with this company. Daimler are suing me for $34,000 for my car that was repossessed a few months ago. What a fabulous day? I am seeking the Lord; I feel I am drowning, and I am not a strong swimmer. Oh to have a normal life and live within the constraints of the law of the land.

25 March, 2004

Wow, another fun-filled week. It started off so well with a 4-day natural horsemanship clinic at our place. It was great to ride the horses and enjoy ourselves. Then Ralph's wedding band arrived in the mail, he had cut it in half. Melody and I shed a few tears. He, aka Sinister, really wants us to experience maximum damage, but all it does is send us running to God and Victory.

One of the ladies that boards her horses with me has just handed me a set of car keys to a second-hand station wagon. She and her husband had purchased me a car! When I said there was no way I could accept it, she assures me it was a spare car they just happened to have. In the midst of turmoil, God sends Victory.

We now start getting into weird stuff. This is the beginning of us realising how bad things have become. Ralph's brother has just returned from spending a weekend with his extended family. Ralph had emailed his sister a photo of himself dressed in leather bondage with a woman standing over him in like attire. This prompts me to dig a little deeper into Ralph's life. On his credit card statements I find out he is a regular at strip clubs. It is so hard for me to grasp the depths of Ralph's fall. I start to wonder how long this has been going on. Has he slept with a prostitute while being married to me? There are so many questions swimming around in my head. He has forsaken God and his family for his own enjoyment. Ralph, the so-called prophet. Ralph, the one God supposedly talks to directly. Ralph, the one who knows his 'calling' and forsook his family to follow it. Where has this man of God gone? I cannot put into words the total and absolute grief I feel for him. I can almost hear him blaming his sexual misdemeanours on me because I refused to submit to his authority. What would have happened if I had moved to Estonia? There is no doubt in my mind at this point, that these sexual endeavours were already in place long before our separation. It scares me to think what could have been, the girls and I living in an apartment, Ralph drinking, working late, bad tempered because we cramp his style. God knew his heart. I now believe the girls and I had sensed this demonic activity while we visited him in Estonia, hence why all three of us were very clear about not moving.

10 April, 2004 - Good Friday

Ralph has come back with another vicious attack. I resigned as the secretary of the company that supposedly owns our property, and as a result he is sending in liquidators to repossess all livestock and equipment. It is beyond comprehension that he would sell his children's ponies. Does he not care? I have had a really tough time dealing with this and I have been very emotional. My lawyer has told me to calm down, to trust him and to trust God. Of course, it all worked out. My lawyer put a stop to it as the horses were Christmas presents and not company assets.

On a more positive note, where Victory stands, a couple that board their horses here have decided they don't want to have to move them, so they are organising the finance to enable them to buy my property. Not only that, but they are not interested in living here so they will rent it back to me. How amazing is God! It has been a year since separation and this year is all about change and new beginnings. It is Easter and Christ died and rose again for us. He is in control and no one else. The crazy thing is, I wanted Ralph to buy the property and rent it back to me, but that would have been very unwise, instead a lovely couple (the ones who gave me the car) bought the property and I still got to rent it back.

24 April, 2004

Ralph has been on the phone to the girls bragging about his new girlfriend, not sure what happened to the other one. This one is 29 and he tells the girls she is an exotic dancer. She is actually a lap dancer from one of the clubs he attends. She has a 22-month-old son. This is the same woman who he is posing with in the photo he sent his sister. The fact that he is sharing all this with the girls is not right. We are still legally married.

20 May, 2004

I have been busy sorting out the house and getting ready for court. Ralph has been rather quiet, which is nice. He has now been diagnosed with chronic fatigue. I find this quite humorous considering he is supposedly the strong one. Our court date is set for next Tuesday but Ralph still hasn't lodged his documents so I doubt it will be going ahead. Last week I had to go to court for a case with Canon Australia, this is due to a debt from one of Ralph's companies. Victory was on point, it was something out of a comedy. My lawyer was so concerned about it but God was in control. Canon's solicitor *was 20 minutes late and it was his first day on the job. Every time he tried asking me a question my lawyer would object. At the end of the hearing the solicitor came over and apologised if he had upset me. Why do we worry when God is in the driver's seat? I was dismissed as the courts acknowledged I had nothing to do with it.*

It has been a tough month financially, having had to pay the school fees has really made us fall behind. Victory yet again: I needed bread for school lunches, and I had \$3, just enough. As I got out of the car I prayed that the bread would be given to me. I walked into the bakery, picked up a loaf of bread and the baker says, "You can have that, it's my last loaf".

It is awesome feeling God's precious, caring love. "Ask and you will receive". I have sold two of Peggy's puppies, which gave me just the right amount to pay my stable hand's wages. "Be faithful in the small things". I now need to pray for the successful sale of the floats and horses. I want all the bits and pieces sorted before the sale of the house. I want to clean out the old, ready for the new. Start afresh.

24 June, 2004

We did go to court. Ralph submitted the documents in the final hour. Court went well according to my lawyer, but it left me a bit flat. The court has ordered that all current outstanding debt of \$800,000 be paid immediately upon the sale of the house. That is the only order that has been given, unfortunately it still *leaves me with all the credit card debts. This will be sorted at a later court date. The next court date is set for July 17, where it will be conducted with a registrar. The clients and the lawyers are present, and everyone fights it out in a room for two hours - something to really look forward to?*

In other news, I sent an email to Ralph explaining why the girls did not want to travel to Estonia to see him. He really does not understand that going to a foreign country, to a dad they no longer know, is not something we should put our kids through. He of course took offence and emailed me all sorts of abuse back. After his attack he calmed down and he realised he needed to speak to the girls more often and started ringing them on a more regular basis. The girls did not like it, as they struggled to communicate with him, but I know it is good for them and how important it is for them to have a relationship with their father.

Now for a good story. My church has a charity event yearly, and I really wanted to contribute. It is hard to know how much to give, when you have no idea how much or how little you will have at the end of a divorce. I prayed and settled on a pledge of $5000. This sounds like a lot, but I felt it probably wasn't enough. Any amount seems huge when you have been told for ten years that churches are ripping you off. A week after this decision I sold a horse float for $7000, and one of the horses for $1000. I sat down to work out my immediate bills. I rang my brother Anton, as he had lent me $2500. He was praying at that precise moment that God would send him cash. God answered my prayer and in turn answered Anton's - but then Sinister disguised as Ralph stepped in.

This all happened simultaneously: the sale of the house went through, and my lawyer received a letter from Ralph's accountant in Hong Kong, suing me for $680,000. I of course, spat the dummy, even though Victory had come through and God had provided miraculously. I am so weak in my faith. Why don't I trust God? He always sees me through. I stressed all night for nothing, as the following day God worked a miracle. You see, the night before, Ralph had rung Jayden for a chat, and Jayden told him what a hard time I was having financially. Ralph was so pleased, that was just what he wanted, for me to suffer so the girls would look to him for money. Except the girls look to God for provision, and not man. Anyway, the miracle was that I was due to spend the day with my lawyer, brainstorming how to fight the claim for $680,000, when Ralph sent an email to Jayden. He completely changed direction. He wanted $150,000 to be sent overseas to be placed in a trust fund for the girls, out of which they can withdraw $1000 per month for education. He will relinquish my liability on all his companies, and the balance of the money goes to me. Ralph's motives for this change of heart are impure, as he wants the girls to believe that all money comes from him. But God's ways are perfect, and the girls know that there is more to life than money. What an amazing outcome: pledge $5000 and receive $500,000 in return.

30 August, 2004

It has been a couple of months since Ralph agreed on the settlement, and I was believing that it was all coming to an end, we were so close. Ralph has changed his mind; he has returned to the thoughts of me not deserving the money. Apparently, I wouldn't look after it well. It would seem that he doesn't want to lose control over me. He knows that once the consent orders are signed, we can both move forward, but I feel he doesn't want that to happen. It saddens me beyond comprehension that he would want the girls and I to be suffering. I only want what's best for him, I want him in sweet communion with the Lord. He wants unhappiness, strife and poverty to fall upon me. I know this will not happen, God is on the throne of my life, my steps are ordered by the Lord. Nothing is done without His consent. What men do for evil, God turns around for His good. Doesn't Ralph understand that the more he hinders my walk the more I run to God? God spoke to me during worship at church, "Trust me, I will see you through. All things will work for good."

How awesome is God, He talks to me? I lost it last Thursday, but I knew having a meltdown is sometimes good for the soul. Scream, yell, sob, cry, get it out, then run to God. He is our only answer.

It hurts. I had plans on starting a travel agency, but it is okay - dreams need to die, if it is to be, then God will see it come to pass. Otherwise, there is something better out there for me. God will show me. It is not easy giving up everything and holding on tight, but it will be worth it in the end. Nothing can replace my relationship with God. I am not saying I am not extremely stressed - but that is normal human behaviour. I do not profess to be some super spiritual giant. I'm not, I'm weak, with a mustard seed of faith. Walking with Jesus is where I will find true life, true meaning, abundance and happiness. Dumb Sinister and Ralph, bring it on - Victory is in control! All things work together for good for those who trust Him.

I was stressing yet again about finances and guess what, Centrelink has put an extra $500 into my account! Praise God, I managed to get all my immediate bills paid. I now have to believe for school fees. God will do it, as only He can.

01 September, 2004 - Spring

My favourite season. My lawyer just called, and it is finally over. Ralph has signed the consent orders; they are on their way from Estonia. It is so hard for me to believe. God is good. My lawyer said, "Don't question it, just know it is an answer from God". At last, I can move forward. Victory, guide my steps. I need wisdom on how to invest the money, it all seems so surreal. Victory let's move on together.

I wish I could say that is the end of the drama and I go on to live a quiet, successful life, but that just isn't the case. Ralph continues to harass me constantly. He will not let go.

Chapter 11

MY BROTHER

I AM ABOUT to embark on the tale of Jayden, aka, younger brother. We have always had a great relationship, but it was mostly based on me helping to bail him out. He was always getting into trouble and thrived on it. People love Jayden, he is very charismatic, loads of fun and highly competitive, especially against his brother. Considering how liked he was, and charming, he certainly did not treat my daughters well. He tolerated Harmony, because she pampered to his needs and fed his ego, however, that was not the case with Melody. Jayden was all about looks, and if you did not fit his mould of attractiveness, he did not have the time for you. He often told Melody that she was ugly and when was she going to fix her teeth? Considering he was her uncle he was very cruel. He told me once when we were young that there was no way I would be able to attract a boyfriend until I had a nose job, as no one wanted a girl with an oversized nose. He is a very shallow person.

This dynamic personality was somehow very appealing to the opposite sex, they found him charming. Jayden had a type: always younger, blonde, with perfect figures, and gentle natured. The women he dated were always gorgeous and unfortunately a lot of them were women I knew. Little Munchkins was a haven for him, there was a dating pool ripe for the picking. It took a while for me to realise why my staff were leaving; they were heartbroken. These girls fell madly in love with him, but for some reason he never committed to them. He moved into the granny flat on my property, but I had to make sure he promised not to date any of the girls that boarded their horses with me. He broke his promise and went ahead and dated one of the girls anyway. He really disappointed me, and yet again this poor girl fell madly in love with him. The relationship did last for a couple of years, but eventually he broke her heart. The fascinating thing with these beautiful women is that even though they were left heartbroken, they always ended up being his friend. To this day he still speaks to a lot of them, and they always speak well of him.

Jayden also struggled to get ahead financially. He had big visions and ideas, but not the financial backing to make it happen. Some of his ideas were brilliant but they needed capital, which is something he didn't have. He tended to spend money way before he had it, and he wanted the best in life. His lifestyle went way beyond his means. It wasn't long before it started to sour financially, and he was in a huge amount of debt. My parents kept providing him with more and more money, but it wasn't helping. There were sheriffs knocking on my parents' front door, demanding money, or coming to assess their assets, because Jayden had made mum secretary of his company – so the debt collectors were coming after her. They received demand notices. My mum ended up being scared to open her front door. She was in the early stages of dementia by this time, so having people knock on the door stressed her out and no doubt exacerbated her condition. The reason why my parents were being targeted was twofold: Jayden had used them as guarantors, and he used my father's name to borrow money. Both their first names started with J, so Jayden would apply using Dad's details.

Jayden was a printer by trade, but he was always distracted with other ideas. He would receive a printing job, with the promise of great income, then print it but not carefully proofread, and inevitably there would be a mistake. He would then have to reprint it and make a loss.

Jayden had a way of attracting trouble. There is just a huge array of shifty happenings that always surrounded him. There was one situation where an acquaintance asked if he could acquire some pills that could be sold for a profit. He was after a thousand of them. Now would you not think that you would immediately say, "No, that is not something I want to be involved in"? Not Jayden, he says, "Let me see what I can find". He asks one of his dodgy friends to contact a drug dealing gangster and see how much it will cost. Typical Jayden doesn't really give this much thought, as he was probably just thinking "Nothing will come of it". Well next minute, his mate has arranged for a thousand pills to be delivered and tells Jayden he has to cough up $23,000 to pay for it. Jayden has no money and has no way of paying off a really scary dude who would not hesitate to dispose of your body. He has to find the money, which he does eventually manage to do, but he cannot pay for the merchandise in one go and he has his life threatened until the debt is paid. Yes, this is crazy stuff, but unfortunately this is not his only encounter with dodgy deals. They continue to come thick and fast throughout his life.

Jayden had an office in the middle of Kings Cross, and of course it was decked out in the finest of furniture; he even had a side business of a spray tan booth. That is because he is very vain, so he had to have brown skin and white teeth at all times. Something very Sinister happened while he had his office in Kings Cross, and my thoughts on this are pure speculation only. He had been given printing film to make plates for an Australian fifty dollar note. I believe he might have been mixed up with the mafia and agreed to print this money. One day he had no money, the next he was flush with cash. He even had a crane brought in to put a spa on the balcony of the unit he rented. He was spending up big time. He didn't go ahead with the job, as he realised what a terrible mistake that would have been, however he now had to pay back the mafia. Impossible, as the money had been spent. What happened next was the last straw for my parents - thugs turned up outside their home and spent the day watching them. My mum's health was struggling and the stress of this was no help. Dad decided the only solution was to sell their home and use some of the money to pay off Jayden's debts and rent a house.

Meanwhile, Jayden's life was being threatened, and he decided to leave Australia and go to Estonia and hang out with Ralph. Those two have always been close. Ralph helped him financially, so the mafia backed off my parents. Really, my brother did actually think printing money was a good plan and absolutely nothing could go wrong.

There was another time when Jayden was supposedly just delivering a print job somewhere in Kings Cross and someone happened to run past him and stab him in the neck. If that was the case, wouldn't you call the police? Not Jayden. He wrapped a towel around his neck, drove to the nearest hospital, rang a friend, waited for them to arrive, and then walked into emergency. The knife had just missed a major artery. He was lucky to be alive. Jayden's life is full of mystery. He never told any of us what he was involved with, so it is all a guessing game.

While Jayden was in Estonia with Ralph, other bizarre things occurred. Ralph was now married to his exotic dancer, and they had a daughter together and lived outside of the capital city in the country on a dilapidated farm that needed renovating. Jayden would go there on weekends and as he had no other friends, he spent a lot of time with Ralph. During these weekends he witnessed Ralph's manic mood swings. The neighbour was a high court judge and he had politely asked Ralph if he could remove his bags of horse manure from the fence line, as the smell was most unpleasant. Ralph took offence and from that point on he started waging a war against his neighbour. He placed rotting fish along the fence line and threw weed killer onto the neighbour's roses and lawn. He was completely unreasonable, all because the neighbour had politely asked him to remove the manure.

The neighbour on the other side of his property complained about the parties that occurred at Ralph's place every weekend and the loud music that was being played until the early hours. Then one day, this neighbour sustained mysterious injuries. Supposedly he had taken a nasty fall from his verandah. Jayden was in shock that this was all happening, but he was now indebted to Ralph and therefore he stayed in Estonia and thought it best to remain friends with Ralph, as clearly becoming an enemy would be a very bad idea.

Eventually Jayden decided he needed a break from all things Estonia, and he chose to fly to Miami as it was somewhere he was interested in going. While in Miami, there was another strange incident. Supposedly he had gone there to buy boats, which in itself is very odd. Boats for what, for whom, and with what money? While there, he sliced his finger while running up the street. The finger was nearly severed. Interestingly it looked like the finger had been cut using something like a cigar cutter. Jayden had to go to a hospital to have stitches, and while there he had some sort of near death experience. He actually died for a couple of minutes, and they had to revive him. Totally bizarre happenings.

Jayden met another beautiful woman in Estonia but this time she fell pregnant. It does surprise me that this is the only girlfriend who had fallen pregnant. He seemed happy over there, and being the way he was, he came up with a brilliant idea, something he'd seen while visiting us to celebrate dad's 60th birthday. He wanted to start an indoor trampoline centre - great idea, but he ended up finding a building and getting side tracked into starting a nightclub instead. Why, might you ask? I have no answers. The nightclub was highly successful though, and he was finally thriving. That is, until the Estonian mafia who owned all the other nightclubs found out how successful he was, and then they were not so happy. Again, he gets caught up with mafia. They threaten him, he doesn't listen, they cause no end of trouble. One night they came in and blocked all the toilets and the place flooded. Jayden had to close it down.

At the time Jayden came home for dad's 60th, his girlfriend, Valerie was 24 weeks pregnant, and decided to stay in Estonia. With her boyfriend on the other side of the world, Valerie went into labour and at 24 weeks, Allie was born. It is hard to imagine being born so early, and in a country where the medical standards were not what we are used to here. Allie survived, though, and today is a thriving seven-year-old. Allie is the Victory in this story. Jayden adores her, and she has changed his life. Immediately after the 60th, Jayden flew back to Estonia to be with his daughter and Valerie. They had a tough few months to contend with, but they came out Victorious.

When Allie was one year old, they all moved back here. It was great having Allie in our lives. Valerie seemed like a lovely person, and ready to calm Jayden down now that he had a family. Sadly, it did not work out that way. Valerie was waiting for the ring, waiting for the commitment of marriage, but Jayden, for whatever reason, never gave her that assurance that marriage brings. They relocated to Queensland,

Jayden continued to struggle financially, yet they tried to live a lavish lifestyle. Valerie started to crack, and Jayden did not treat her well. He was paranoid she would become fat in her old age, and he could not have a wife who wasn't perfect to look at. It is sad to say but she started having an affair. Their relationship disintegrated and Valerie moved in with the new man. Valerie turned nasty as she wanted full custody for Allie, and she was not going to accept anything less.

While waiting for the custody court case there just so happened to be an incident at Jayden's home. A Molotov bottle was thrown at his home and his car. The car caught on fire and was a total write off. It was never proven who did this. Jayden was also running his business out of the home at the time, and suddenly, the real estate agent came over and explained he was not allowed to run a business from this rental. At the court hearing Valerie accused Jayden of child neglect, stating that Allie was never in bed before eleven at night and was fed McDonalds for dinner most nights. This was not the truth, and she was caught out in a lot of lies. Jayden was awarded 10 days out of 12. Valerie was livid. The sad thing is that Jayden did not want full custody, he was happy to have 50-50, but she was determined to have only full custody. They have been to court three times and each time it has cost Jayden a crazy amount of money, and each time he wins. It saddens me that children are always the innocents in these battles. Allie has done nothing wrong, but she is the one who must be the grown-up, to love both parents and to adjust to living in two very different homes.

It seemed that after years of Jayden doing the wrong thing by everyone, the tables had now turned.

He is a great father, and Allie has really matured him as he now has the responsibility of raising a child. He adores his daughter and will do anything for her. It is so good to see.

There are so many layers to the stories about Jayden, but he has kept most of them close to his chest. I can continue to speculate about his dodgy dealings and just what Ralph has over him, but it is just that, speculation. What I can say is he is not the same man as he was before Allie. His only priority now is his daughter. I really do hope that the days of drug deals, stabbings and mafia are over. I wish him true joy and happiness.

Chapter 12

THE YEARS IN BETWEEN

I WAS HOPING Victory would take full control after the divorce, but we have to accept that Sinister is always on the prowl, trying to cause maximum damage. Ralph had set up an overseas trust fund for the girls, which was to provide them with funds for anything they needed, as well as pay their school fees. For a while this was exactly what happened, and now that I think about it, it was probably while the money he received from the divorce was available - but once that ran dry, he started to put demands on sending the money. There were lots of emails backwards and forwards explaining that you did not just get given money, you had to earn it. If the girls wanted money, they had to send him regular emails with details on what they had been up to, and photos. We are now talking about teenagers, though. They do not do what is required by a demanding bully of a father, they live their life. He then blamed me for being a bad parent and not teaching the teenagers that it is rude to not correspond fully with their father, who was also their bank. The next thing to disappear was the funds to pay their school fees. This time it was because they did not send him a Father's Day card or contact him. Interesting how it was okay for him to forget Melody's birthday, but not okay for them to not acknowledge him. Let's be honest, he had not been a great father and the relationship was very strained between the three of them. The games of manipulation that he used on me as a teenager were not going to work on these two strong and capable girls. It was still extremely hard for the girls to be constantly told they were doing the wrong thing. Melody was a peacemaker and she tried so hard to keep him happy, but it was never enough.

Ralph came back and stayed for a month in October, at a local caravan park with his partner and her son. The plan was for the girls to stay with them for two weeks and I was very much looking forward to some alone time. It was not to be, though. After a couple of days, the girls started to fall apart. Their father was supposed to be a strong Christian man with morals, loving and encouraging, but he was not that, and it came as a shock to them. He was aggressive, he had started smoking, and the ridiculous thing is he would have to have his Ventolin in hand while he smoked. He constantly badmouthed me and tried to get the girls to side with him, but the last straw was when his partner's three-year-old son went to drink from a popper juice that looked like water in the fridge, but it was actually vodka. How very Russian of him. The girls were distraught and not knowing what to do, they locked themselves in the bathroom and rang me. I went and picked them up; he was not happy. I was threatened because I was breaking court orders, and he told the girls they were weak and needed to grow up. I prayed that Victory would take charge and there would be no consequences for us because we had broken court orders. He didn't take it to court, but he most certainly made sure we knew that our behaviour was unacceptable.

The three of us were so distressed by all of this that we decided to travel to Malaysia. Within three days we were on our way. Now I know this is not great, as it is true Ralph was supposed to have the girls, but they would not go back and stay with him. The girls were old enough to decide this, and if one thing is for sure, you cannot force a teenager. They said if I sent them back, they would just get a taxi and come home. The girls had told their dad they would see him when they returned from their holiday. We had a wonderful time away. We saw the orangutans and the hatching of turtles. It was an enjoyable break from all the chaos. Unfortunately, when we returned home, the girls still did not want to see their dad. They had organised to spend the day with him, but Harmony decided to go to a friend's place, and Melody opted to come to a conference I was attending, to participate in the teen girls' program. Ralph knew he couldn't manipulate Harmony, so he left her alone, but Melody was still young enough and she had a soft heart. He refused to let her go. She went anyway, and during the conference he turned up to take her and I panicked. I was called out of my program and rather than calmly see what was happening I called the police. Not very smart of me. Ralph had an unhealthy dislike of authority, so he was not impressed. The police explained to him that there was nothing he could do as Melody was old enough to refuse to get into the car. What was supposed to be an enjoyable day turned into a disaster. I am grateful he was living overseas, otherwise this sort of thing would occur on a regular basis. A couple of days after this incident he flew away.

There are so many incidents throughout the years that kept Sinister alive and active, mostly using Ralph to wreak havoc. He had spies everywhere and he took great pride in informing me that he was aware of what I was up to at all times. I did not know who I could trust. It is not a nice way to live. The hardest thing to accept is that my brothers believed I deliberately sabotaged the girls' relationship with their father, and that I was doing my best to drive a wedge between them. I tried to encourage the girls to contact him and send him photos, but they really did not know who this man was. This was not the father they grew up with. My brothers placed all the blame on me. When you are going through a crisis you believe you can always rely on family, but not me. Still to this day, many years later, they keep in contact with Ralph. Even my father insists on answering Ralph's phone calls and visiting him.

This is one example of the sort of emails the girls might have received from their dad. Firstly, his secretary sent them an email informing them that their father, along with his partner, had been mugged, and they were okay but had to go to hospital. The next email was from Ralph, and this is what he wrote. "I just found out that Lisa sent you an email to say that I was mugged last Monday. Yes, this is true, but I was going to wait until we were all better before I told you, and after the dramas the week before I didn't think it was the right time. Anyway, we are now okay, just a little blue in the eyes, a few body bruises and seven stitches in my head. There were three of them, and one of them ended up in hospital the next day with a broken leg, so we are almost even, one down and two to go." He then sent them a photo of his face, completely battered. He actually put in writing to his children that the muggers were being taken care of. A later email suggested one was no longer with us.

I need to explain my daughters' personalities before progressing to the next story. Harmony came across as strong, capable, an encourager, very organised and extremely loyal. Ralph adored her from the second she was born. He highly favoured her and spoilt her rotten. If Harmony asked for something she would get it. When she was 16, she asked for his support in sending her to Austria on an exchange program, and he provided the funds. She had to promise he could visit her, but that didn't happen. Melody on the other hand, was the second girl, and he really wanted a boy, so she just did not get the same attention. Melody also looked like me, while Harmony's looks favoured his family. Melody is a gentle soul, loving, kind, silly and fun-loving. Her personality was not as appealing to Ralph as Harmony's. He would still provide things for her, but it always came with an expectation. Melody tried for years to get her father to love her, but after meeting him for dinner when she was 17 and listening to him tear her to shreds, justifying his actions and placing blame on her innocent shoulders, she gave up. Both girls stopped all communication with him and have not spoken a word to him since. You might think that this is harsh and unfair, after all he is their father, but they needed to distance themselves from this toxic relationship. They have both forgiven him for his neglect, but they cannot enjoy a relationship with him without his manipulation taking control.

When Melody was 12, she wanted to improve her horse riding and wanted a weekly natural horsemanship lesson. As she didn't want to place any financial burden on me, she decided to ask her dad. He gave her some complicated explanation of where her trust money comes from and how all money spent needed to be appropriately recorded. He would agree to pay for the lessons, however she had to provide a weekly report with photos and videos. Such a lot of rubbish. She agreed, but she was young, and it wasn't long before she did not send him weekly reports. Ralph took matters into his own hands and decided to track down her instructor. He found out the instructor was not working under the natural horsemanship company he assumed she worked for and yet again he was livid. Picture this: father rings daughter, she happily chats to him, he starts to get aggressive and accuses her of lying, that her instructor did not even work for Natural Horsemanship. Melody tried to explain that she still taught the same content but was not with them as it was not necessary. He then screams at her that she was not even getting lessons and that she lied, so he would send her the money and then give it to me. I watched my daughter, sobbing, trying to explain herself, but he was not listening, and she collapsed on the floor. It was so hard to watch.

This girl was kind and gentle and she was being crushed with accusations by her father. It is a true testament to her character that she still spent a further five years trying to have a relationship with him.

Sinister wanted to try a new angle; I think he realised that the girls and I were standing up to Ralph's demands and his influence was waning. The lovely couple who purchased the property wanted me to move out, as they had a friend who wanted a place to stay. I thought it was a great idea for us to move on, start afresh somewhere, but it was not going to be as straightforward as I had hoped. We had a menagerie, including dogs, cats, ducks and horses. I believed Victory would come through for us. We started packing and looking for a rental. It took five long, stressful months; we were pretty much squatting but because we had nowhere to go the landlords could not kick us out. Every weekend was spent walking through rentals, then putting in applications. Every Monday we were rejected as I was a single mum with too many animals. It was soul destroying. We managed to find a lovely paddock for the horses, so we had only to find a place for the rest of us. Having owned my homes for so many years I had no idea how hard it was to rent. Eventually after living in a house full of packed boxes, we were finally approved for a house. Victory did come through, just a bit slower than we would have liked. The reason they rented to us was because the lease was only six months, not the usual 12, and the place had a python that lived in the roof. I had no problem with either issue, I was happy to just have a home and I had no issues with snakes. We ended up living here for seven years, and it was the perfect home for us. It was close to the local shopping centre and to the cinema. Both girls worked at the cinema which was a great job but with a mean boss. The house was huge, with six bedrooms, two lounge rooms and a massive kitchen and dining area. It was owned by a development company with plans to eventually bulldoze it and subdivide the land. As the house was rather large, we filled the spare rooms up with boarders. This meant there was always a houseful of people, so you could never be lonely.

We had a lot of fun in this home. Harmony had her 16th birthday party here, for which she hired a juke box with karaoke. I was banned from attending and banished to my room. I decided to disguise myself by putting on a pink wig, some sort of crazy outfit, and large glasses. Her friends thought it was hilarious, Harmony not so much. Harmony also had her 21st birthday in this house. This time she sent out invites that looked like movie tickets. We organised a hotdog stand and a popcorn machine. We had a friend put up a large timber board as a movie screen, and we hired a projector. Everyone sat outside on blankets with pillows watching movies. We even had fireworks - which I admit were illegal. Unfortunately, when they were lit, one fell over, which set all of them off. There were fireworks going left, right and centre. A good illustration of why they were illegal. Could have been a disaster, so we were lucky the police were not called.

For one of Melody's earlier birthdays, I set up a table at the end of the yard full of disgusting food items, including custard, jelly, cream, and anything that was wobbly. It was a massive food fight, with so much mess, so much laughter. Unfortunately, we didn't think about the dogs, who spent the day licking up the mess; they were very quiet for a few days after that.

We often had young people over and I just became one of the crowd. Often, we would scream around the place shooting each other with Nerf gun bullets. We also ran a youth connect group, where we shared our walk with Jesus with them, and encouraged them on life's journey. Our doors were always open.

Our dog Peggy, the Airedale, was constantly escaping and it was proving to be a problem. There was a high school close by and she would run over there, play football with them, then help herself to lunches she found in school bags. I was constantly having to go pick her up. Even though our home was fenced, she worked out she could walk through the massive water pipe and get out. I started locking her in the house, but she learnt to open doors by putting her paws on the door handle and walking backwards on two legs, so we now had to lock the doors. Next, she learnt how to open windows! There was no stopping her. Our new plan was to lock her in the pool area. She was still escaping but we had no clue how, so we videoed her. Turns out she would launch herself at a tree, swing her legs over a branch, and shimmy up the branch until she could launch herself over the fence. If we hadn't videoed it, we would never have believed this was possible. A lady that looked after the gardens of a nearby property started to pick her up off the streets for me, and eventually we gave her to this lady, as she could take Peggy to work with her and prevent all this escaping. The problem was, Peggy had always lived on our property and always had people around, but when we moved away, she could not cope with being alone all day. She was an exceptional dog, very clever.

Chapter

13

THE TRAVEL DREAM

I MENTIONED IN a previous chapter that I had a dream to start a travel agency. When I was just 17, I had written in my journal that I wanted to start this agency in my own suburb. And that is exactly what I did. It was 20 years later that my desire became a reality. I had just attended a women's conference titled Women Dreaming, and we were encouraged to write down our dreams no matter how outrageous they seemed. I wrote "start a travel agency", but I did not tell a soul. The following year's conference theme was The Journey, and throughout the conference an image of a plane, a suitcase and a passport was projected on the big screen. It was all about travel. Victory was being very clear about hinting what my next step was to be.

One day I was driving the girls past the local shops and there was a new shop being built, and I just declared that was going to be my office. The girls had no idea I wanted to start a travel business; they thought I had lost the plot. This was the time in our lives when Ralph was threatening to destroy me financially and hold up our settlement in the courts for years. I had no idea how I was going to see this dream come to pass, but God always has a way, and He hears the desires we whisper to Him in our darkest hours. I rang the landlord and told him I was tied up with a settlement and I wasn't sure how long it would take. He was willing to wait as he thought my business would go well in the space. Three months later I opened my doors. My agency had been birthed. What a huge learning curve I had before me! I had not worked in the industry for over 10 years and a lot had changed in that time. I painted my office pink and furnished it to match my personality. I could make all the decisions as this was my own project. It was all very exciting. It didn't take long for me to learn all the new procedures; it was exhilarating using all this brain capacity.

It was important for me to not only provide my clients with professional service, but also that I build a strong relationship with them. I wanted to make sure I was available for clients and friends. I purchased a coffee machine so I could provide cappuccino and lattes to everyone. The office became a place where you were always welcome, and I was always happy to stop to listen. I have been honoured to share life's journey with many who are heart-broken, lost and confused. From a young age I wanted a travel agency, but I also wanted to be available to help others, and I was doing both. The girls would catch the bus from school to the office and do their homework there. I tried to make sure I wasn't too busy to hear about their days. Parenting my daughters was still my number one priority. The horses were boarded just down the road, and they were cheeky Haflingers. I was often called as they would break free from their paddocks and go help themselves to the neighbourhood gardens. My community was getting to know me, not just through my business but also through my naughty ponies.

Owning your own business sounds so romantic and of course a walk in the park, and how I wish that was so. As many people know, the reality of owning a business is hard work, a lot of stress and a constant challenge. Added to that was the fact that my travel agency was located in a small suburb, in an industry that was challenging. While it's a huge amount of fun if it's your passion - which of course it was for me - it doesn't reap huge financial rewards. We poor agents work very hard for very little return, and there were many expenses - rent, licences, utility bills, wages, the normal daily running of a business. I had months of great abundance and others of very little, just like in any business. Victory showed up repeatedly, always at the last second, to provide for our financial needs. I always managed to push through to another year. Until disaster struck - but you'll have to wait as all will be explained in a later chapter.

In the travel industry we are blessed to have the opportunity to, of course travel - both for work and for pleasure. In order for me to do this I needed staff to take care of things while I was away, and they needed to be paid. Staff can be tricky as they generally don't work as hard as you, and that can be a challenge for a boss. My first year in business I had a friend come in once a week just to give me a break, and in the second year I employed another friend three days a week. The tricky part was that I wasn't busy enough to employ someone full time and I didn't need someone who was necessarily qualified in the industry, as I was happy to train them. I did need someone who was a quick learner, though, and had great customer service. Over the years I managed to employ over 10 people, some were amazing and others quite a challenge. A couple of them have become wonderful friends and I am forever grateful that they are a part of my life. One staff member accidentally booked a flight on the wrong date, for a 17-year-old who was returning home from Germany after attending a ballet school on a scholarship. The student was supposed to be flying home in October but was accidentally booked to return after Christmas. My staff member did not handle it well and resigned and left me to find a solution. Another was secretly booking trips for all her family and friends minus the commission. She was extremely busy and brought a lot of business through the door, but the business wasn't making any money because she was giving them the net price. Then there was my favourite: I had decided to employ a junior full time and give someone young and inexperienced an opportunity to be in the travel industry. This one came up with so many excuses for sick days, and while some were genuine, others were very creative. "My boyfriend yelled at me", "I locked my car keys in my apartment", "My grandmother needs me", "I vomited on the way to work so I need to go home", "I have a bad period", "My now-ex-boyfriend's new girlfriend yelled at me on the street", and my absolute favourite, "I topless sun-baked over the weekend and got burnt so I cannot wear a bra". I believe that she had 18 sick days in six months. Before her year of training was up, she quit because her life was too stressful. All the staff I have had the privilege of employing have had something to offer and I know it wasn't easy for them to be a part of my crazy life. There was always some drama transpiring in the background and at times they had to carry me when I had to deal with unexpected situations. I appreciate them all and thank them for standing by me. All of my staff left of their own accord for various reasons. There was no bad blood for which I am grateful.

As a travel professional it is very important that I travel the globe - I know, it is a tough gig. There is no point being in this industry if you don't travel, and the more travelling you do, the better you are at your job. I have experienced so many amazing places, so I will highlight a few that come to mind.

Many of my personal trips were with Liz, who is my oldest friend and the Godmother of my children. Liz was with me when I gave birth to Harmony. Liz's husband wasn't a traveller and so he loved it when he could send Liz off on an adventure with me. Our first massive adventure was to Morocco. What a great country. Morocco took me by surprise, as it was fascinating and so colourful. Mosaics, donkeys, deserts, delicious food, markets, spices, leather, ceramics, unknown sights, and smells. A delightful place.

We also travelled together to Alaska on a small ship adventure, where we kayaked amongst whales and saw black bears from a distance. Unlike Morocco, which was a very low budget, this trip was high end. We would travel out on the zodiacs (inflatable boats) to look at glaciers and while observing we would be served hot chocolate laced with deliciousness. We were very spoilt and decided that if possible, all our trips should be of this standard.

Another time we cruised on a small ship on the Mekong from Vietnam into Cambodia. We loved this small ship cruising, so we booked ourselves on another in Europe that went from Budapest to Amsterdam. These trips with Liz were always such great fun, we were great travelling companions. The last trip we went on together before disaster struck the world was to Tuscany. We booked ourselves on a seven-night horse riding holiday. We stayed in this amazing Tuscan villa where all our organic meals were cooked for us, and every day we rode horses all over Tuscany. This trip is one of the highlights of my life. At the end of the day I could barely walk, all of me was numb from kilometres on horseback, but it was incredible. The horses I rode were so well behaved. It was a unique experience and a huge accomplishment. After the week we went on a cruise through Croatia, Mykonos and Santorini. It was enjoyable but a totally different experience to small ship cruises. On this cruise I had the unpleasant experience of a naked man coming into the sauna with me. Liz was in hysterics and thought it was very amusing. There were many moments on our trips that entertained her. There was a flight where a rather large lady sat next to me and proceeded to arrange her hot meal that she had packed for herself on my tray table. Then there was the moment that a gentleman, while he slept and snored on a flight, decided it was a grand idea to grab my thigh. I always seemed to be the one attracting these people, while Liz just sailed on through enjoying my discomfort.

Liz wasn't my only travelling companion; I was also able to take my girls on many trips. There was a river cruise with Melody while Harmony was in Austria on an exchange program. A trip to Las Vegas and Disneyland for Harmony's 18th. An adventure to Hawaii, Phuket, and Israel and Jordan for Melody's 21st. A lot of great memories. I feel that Victory allowed us to travel extensively as a family so we could enjoy all these happy memories. Celebrating Harmony's 21st and Melody's 18th was our most memorable trip by far. It was a total surprise for the girls. I gave them a list of what to pack but refused to tell them where we were going. When we checked in at the airport their boarding passes only said Los Angeles, so they thought we were going to Disneyland. When we landed in Los Angeles, we had to take a connecting flight to New York. Then they got excited: I had purchased tickets to see Taylor Swift at Madison Square Gardens and we were going to be in New York for the Thanksgiving Day parade and Black Friday sales. I feel very blessed to have been able to take my girls away. I was a busy working mum, so being able to travel with them and spend time experiencing the world with them was truly Victory at work. When the girls met their life partners, we dragged them along with us. We all went to Phuket, where Harmony got engaged, and the five of us all went to America, Canada and Hawaii one year over Christmas.

I have also been blessed with many work-related trips. Broome, San Francisco, Hawaii, Hollywood for Halloween, Europe, Kenya, Canada to ski, and a car rally in New Zealand. Work trips are non-stop, with no time for jet lag, but they are incredible because they want to impress, so you manage to experience things you would never normally be able to afford. Skiing all the major resorts of Canada with ski lessons included, dining on the top of a mountain covered in snow, helicopter rides in Hawaii over volcanoes, hot air ballooning in the Serengeti, fine dining and wine tasting in private cellars. The different accommodations I experienced were also out of this world; five-star resorts in the penthouse, safari lodges like Karen Blixen Camp, cabins on cruises that came with a butler, places with outstanding views of oceans and mountains and wild animals. Wherever possible, we were upgraded to fly business class which is truly the only way to fly. It is hard to travel in economy once you have been up the front of the plane!

The travel business is hard, as there is so much to know, and it is so easy to make a mistake which could have detrimental consequences on your clients. Everything must be tripled-checked, and you need to remember so much, like passport validities and transfers and visas, and making sure all the dates match up, so being super aware of different time zones. It is exacting and exhausting work, with little financial gain, but if you love it, it is so rewarding. How can you complain about a job that sends people on holidays that they have been dreaming about for years? The perfect honeymoon, the ideal family getaway, and the adventure of a lifetime. Unfortunately, it is a career that is very reliant on world events, so when disaster hits the world, travel comes to a grinding halt. Swine flu, terrorist attacks, civil unrest, financial collapses, volcanoes, earthquakes, fires and floods - all these influence travel plans, and it is our job to rearrange holidays and even organise to get people home after they've been stranded overseas. This of course has an impact on the bottom line; however, I love this job. What I really need is a rich husband so I can just do this job for the love of it, and not have to worry about the financial side of things. When you are passionate about something, it is a joy to go to work.

GIRLS, HOMES,
BOARDERS AND WEDDINGS

T HE GIRLS AND I settled into the rhythm of life, school
for them and work for me. Ralph often sent me
nasty text messages or emails. Years after our divorce
he would still send something. I think he just wanted
me to know he was still in control. I never responded
to these, which I am sure sent him crazy. Harmony
often struggled through school, a lot of which was her
own doing as she would do the bare minimum. During
her senior years, a teacher came alongside her and
really encouraged her to do well. In fact, this teacher
inspired Harmony to become a teacher herself. After
she graduated high school, she enrolled in a private
college located two hours away. Harmony enjoyed the

university life and moved into one of the girls' dormitories. Here she became a head student which involved keeping an eye on fellow students and their wellbeing. During these years she met her now husband. Harmony is a brilliant teacher, loves all her students and thrives on her organisational skills. She lets students know that even if school might be a struggle that does not mean you cannot be successful.

Melody was, and still is, an over-achiever. She thrives on studying. During her final years at school, it was hard to get her to do anything but study. Melody did so well in her exams she was accepted into Melbourne university to study science and then veterinary science. Again, she excelled in her studies and is today a very competent vet. Melody was introduced to her now husband while she was studying for her high school certificate. However, her boyfriend was studying to be a doctor in Melbourne which meant the distraction was pretty minimal for both of them. Their first twelve months of dating was mostly via telephone calls.

The girls started dating their boyfriends six weeks apart and the funny thing is that they also married these men six weeks apart. We had to organise two weddings in close succession. Harmony was married in December and Melody in January. Both weddings were destination weddings, which just added to the chaos. Harmony and Mitchell were married in the Hunter Valley and Melody and Ken were married at Sutton Forest in the Southern Highlands. Both weddings were stunningly beautiful but very different. Just like my girls.

Harmony and Mitchell's wedding was located in a vineyard. There was a delightful wooden church, vines and a beautiful stone reception building. After the church ceremony, while the happy couple went off for photos, we were offered nibbles while mingling. We were then spoilt with an amazing sit-down meal served with wine from their vineyard. Victory was hovering over all of us that day and it was a wonderful occasion. There was, however, one small issue hanging over our heads; Sinister needed us to know he was never far away. Ralph had informed his father that he was flying in from Estonia and attending the wedding. Harmony was extremely worried he would turn up and ruin her special day. At the time I was friends with a gentleman who was a qualified security officer. He was my 'plus-one' at the wedding and was able to reassure Harmony that he would take care of anyone who intended to cause trouble. Ralph even went so far as to send a screen shot of himself checking in at Dubai airport. In the end this was all a scam, he did not fly to Australia, and he did not attend the wedding. He just loves to make an impact.

Melody's wedding was outstanding, but I must admit it was a lot more work than her sister's. This wedding was outside on the most gorgeous grounds. The theme was all things vintage, even the wedding dress had a vintage three quarter length look to it. The set up for this event was next level. We had to assemble two white wooden doors that Melody walked through as part of the outside aisle. The reception was on the grass, and we set it up with blankets and pillows. There were old books, shelves, cane chairs, an old typewriter and so much bunting. When we transported it all, it was like we were moving house. My most precious friends, Stefan and Bettina, went above and beyond to help with the carting down of everything and the setting up. I have to say, we cannot do life without precious friends, as these two friends of mine have always supported me and my daughters. Melody and Ken had set up giant Jenga, sack races and giant chess. It resembled an English picnic for aristocrats, with high tea. Another delightful wedding.

The year before these weddings my parents had lost their home and they were paying a fortune on a small rental property. They were going to burn through the small amount of money they received from the sale of their house quickly, leaving them no money to retire with. I also was paying a large sum in rent. So we decided to buy a house together. Mum was starting to deteriorate with dementia, so we thought a house together would be a great idea. We eventually found a home that was set up as a dual occupancy. Downstairs had two bedrooms and upstairs had four. It had been on the market for sale for a long time, the owners lived overseas, and the current tenants did not want to move out. We went over to inspect it and there was washing hung all over the house and the verandah was covered in dog poop. The tenant refused to leave the house while we looked and really wanted us to know just how many brown snakes they had found in the house. I laughed and told them I loved snakes and often picked up the diamond pythons from off the hay bales. We managed to buy this house at an incredible price, way below the asking price. Unfortunately, the tenants had a signed agreement and did not have to move out for another six months, so we had to negotiate a sum of money for them to move. It was cheaper than my parents and I renting our current homes. We lived in this house for nearly eight years. My parents put up the deposit and I paid the mortgage. Victory was very much in control here, as it wasn't always easy to find the money for the mortgage due to my business struggling at times, but I never skipped a payment. It really is a miracle. I loved this home. The way it was designed made it easy to keep clean and it had a lovely ambience about it. The only true negative was that it faced the wrong way which meant the sun didn't shine down upon us in winter. I loved that the downstairs area was just as nice as upstairs. It was a perfect arrangement. I filled up my spare rooms with boarders to help cover the mortgage and to keep me company. The year before Harmony married, she moved in to help cover my expenses, and a couple of years after her marriage they moved in yet again to help with my mortgage. Victory always provided a way. This didn't mean Sinister left us alone, far from it. I had the opportunity to buy a house with my parents, but my eldest brother believed this should have been his opportunity, not mine - after all he is the eldest. He accused me of stealing the inheritance. I was a bit confused as my parents were very much alive, so there was no stealing going on, and on top of that my brother was moving six hours away and my parents did not want to move that far. There was a lot of family tension. Let's just put the family drama aside; I had a home which I never thought I would have again, as did my parents. It was a win-win situation for us.

Victory is definitely the one I want to walk me through this life, but Sinister is always on the prowl to try and take us out. I must deal with the Sinister, but I am very aware that Victory has the control. Ralph cannot allow us to move on. Just when you think he has, he will send a message letting you know he is always in control. He managed to find yet another financial loophole in the system: he would apply for a credit card with a $20,000 limit, falsifying the information. Once it was approved, he would fly back here, pick up the card from the bank and then fly out within a couple of days. He had no intention of paying them back. This was his income stream. He arrived once with his young daughter, expecting our girls to want to see her. In other words, it was a ploy, to manipulate them into seeing him. The girls really wanted to see their stepsister, but they knew it would come with expectations. Supposedly the stepsister was distraught when she was here, teary and missing her mother, and Ralph had to leave in a hurry to get her back to her mum.

Ralph had so many health scares over the years, and he felt the need to share these with me. Soon after he left to go live in Estonia, he diagnosed himself with ADHD - attention deficit hyperactivity disorder - which then gave him an excuse for his behaviour. Next diagnosis was a heart attack. He rang me apologising for his behaviour, but the heart attack was in fact a pulled muscle in his shoulder. I believe he was officially diagnosed with bipolar, which explains a lot. Fast forward a few years, and yet again he diagnosed himself with stage four fibrosis/cirrhosis of the liver. He apparently only had six months to live. This one could have been true because over the years, drinking from the moment he woke to the moment he slept, was nearly a daily occurrence. When this medical condition arose, he and his new family had settled in Queensland. Supposedly things were not going well for them in Estonia, in other words he had burnt all his bridges and had decided to return to Australia. He messaged me asking that I inform the girls, which of course I did. Both the girls were hesitant to contact him as he was not to be trusted. It was very hard for them, but they decided to wait until they had received a proper medical report. After a biopsy he was indeed diagnosed with fibrosis of the liver - but only stage one. If he stopped drinking and kept a healthy lifestyle, he could make a full recovery. He does stop drinking for short periods of time, but it doesn't take long before the urge to drink again takes control. It is usually during one of his binges that he messages me. It amazes me how much he remembers from our past, things I have long forgotten. He would have a much better life if he would just move on. I do wonder what his wife thinks with him always obsessing about us.

Over the years I often took on boarders to help pay the rent or mortgage, and there were some real characters and funny moments. There was the woman who had a mouse run up the inside of her jeans. She stripped out of those pants so fast. And the guy who was happy to prance around our home in boxer shorts; the girls were not impressed. There was one who liked her dog a little bit too much; the girl who baked bread and always made us feel hungry; and the guy who opened the bathroom door on a young innocent boarder with nothing on and left her traumatised. I had one lady who only lasted two days. She was livid because one of the house mates had not picked her up when he drove past her walking to the bus stop. He didn't even see her. There was this one couple that clashed with Harmony as she has a strong personality which matched theirs. Another boarder brought a person home to stay a couple of days because they had nowhere to stay. He then went off to his girlfriend's place for a couple of nights and just assumed this extra person had left. When he returned, he found this guy still in his room. He had been sneaking food out of our pantry when no-one was home. There was the time a boarder invited his parents to stay for a couple of weeks - without asking me first! They took over my home and I felt like I was the uninvited guest. One of my favourite boarders was helping me charge the battery to my car one day; he connected the jumper leads to my car and then his, but he had forgotten to take his car out of gear. So, when he leant in and turned on the ignition, his car lurched forward and came so close to careening off the embankment. His car hit a railing, a garbage bin and a couple of large pot plants. He literally wrote off his car. Plus, he hurt himself trying to jump into his car to turn it off. That was an expensive day!

There was never a dull moment in our home. We had people from all over the world - Canada, Switzerland, Indonesia, Darwin, and locals. At times it was challenging as it was never your own space, but it really helped with expenses, you were never lonely, and there was always something interesting going on. I felt honoured to have them in my life, I spent a large portion of time helping them with life choices, discussing dating and college and other major decisions. It was at times a challenge, but it was also a privilege to share life with others and encourage them on their journey.

Chapter 15

SINGLE AND DATING

T HE YEAR WAS 2014 and both girls were engaged. I was busy working and life had settled into a nice even groove. Victory was front and centre. Then Jed walked into my office. We had first met at a women's conference where he was doing security duties, about six years prior. He was friendly and chatty - but very much married at the time. After that we would occasionally bump into him at church, and he had even booked a couple of flights through my travel agency. I hadn't seen him for over three years, but never really gave him much thought. Anyway, one day he came into my office, explaining that he was picking his girls up from school, but he was early so he thought he would pop in and say hi. Nice of him, we chatted for a few minutes. He asked if I had a new man in my life, and I just laughed. He then announced that he was divorced. Oh no. This is a problem. It was fine when he was out of bounds, but he was now single, and I could fall badly. After all he was charming, funny, sensitive, but also not afraid to give me a hard time, and he was very good looking. I really didn't want this door to be opened; I was damaged goods, way too complicated to be with. He had not been attending church for some time, so I invited him to come the following Sunday. He came but did not sit with us. Harmony went into overdrive and had us walking down the aisle before 'hello'.

We chatted a few times on the phone and he managed to squeeze out of me that I had not been on a first date since I was fifteen and had not kissed anyone for eleven years. He thought that was hilarious and how could that even be possible. As if I had men lining up at my door since my divorce. Harmony invited him over for dinner the following week. It went really well; Melody had composed 21 questions and he answered them without too much bloodshed. Things were progressing, but it is hard to gauge where you stand with someone, and let's be honest - I was way out of practice. I was a young girl last time I dated, and now I had two engaged daughters.

It was Harmony's birthday and Jed's the following day, so we decided to all meet up in the city and go out to Jamie's Italian restaurant. We enjoyed a great meal, but the entire time he made sure his leg was touching mine. I was so nervous. He had caught the train in, so I drove him home. Great, I thought, some time alone, but he did not talk much during the drive, and it was only 15 minutes to his place. He invited me in (oh dear), typical me thinks "finally we can chat and really start to get to know each other". His apartment was so cluttered, there was stuff everywhere, and as I squeezed down his hallway filled with overflowing bookshelves, I arrived at the lounge room and behold, a tiny sofa. I was expected to sit there and with no other seats he had to sit next to me. I was quite nervous and couldn't keep still. He enjoyed my pain and watched me squirm. "What's the matter? We are just friends!" I relax. Friends. We are just going to watch *Amazing Race* and talk; I can do that. That would have been simple, but as we all know my life is not simple. He leaned in and started full-on kissing me. Total and utter freak out. I was shaking and tense and not having fun. This was not what I was expecting. He finally backed off, told me to relax - and then leaned in for more. It was so awkward, I felt so uncomfortable. He just went from zero to a hundred in three seconds. We don't even know each other and what happened to friends? Right, it must be friends with benefits. I finally untangled myself from his lips and made my excuse to leave and bolted out the door. He messaged me on the way home with thanks for a fun night. Fun night for whom? No surprises, I did not sleep, the nightmare was on repeat. I could not believe I allowed that to happen. Where did my confidence go? I was way out of my depth and really did not enjoy it. How could I make out with someone when I hardly knew them? He messaged me again the following morning saying thank you for dinner and the birthday present.

Two entire weeks later he finally phoned me, and during those two weeks I overthought everything. Sinister was in my ear, saying "What is wrong with you, he was only kissing you. This is 2014 not the 1800's. People make out on the first date, and it is common practice to sleep with someone you aren't actually dating." I needed to gain confidence and make it clear what I wanted and what I didn't. Call me old fashioned but I believe in spending time with someone and making sure you are compatible before muddling it all up with lust. Sinister also made sure I was aware that Jed had not contacted me in that time, whispering things like "You are not pretty, you didn't give out, you are not worthy. Ralph told you that you were useless, and you are." I needed to sort myself out or this dating thing was going to get way too complicated. Anyway, the phone conversation was great, we had a great chat and I told him what I was feeling. He assured me that he liked me otherwise he would not have invited me into his apartment. Now I was excited, as I had someone who liked me.

I wish I could say that Victory was all over this new relationship but no, Sinister took control. I believed Jed was interested in me and we were heading towards something official. I was so happy and believed it was the perfect timing to start a relationship. I was sharing my news with a friend, and she was so happy for me. Sharing my news, however, was the downfall of this very short-lived relationship. This friend was out for coffee, and one of her friends was saying how she had met this guy, and how happy she was. They were not officially dating yet, but it was only a matter of time. You guessed it; Jed was the guy. He was adamant that he was not seeing anyone else, but the fact that another woman believed there could be something happening was not a good sign.

We kept in contact over the coming year, but the

relationship just didn't happen. He wanted very different things to me. This on-and-off relationship was what enabled me to ask him to my daughter's weddings as my plus-one and as security. He strung me along but there was no substance to him. We drifted apart and I had to understand that it was not meant to be. I took it hard as I really thought Victory had brought Jed into my life. What I came to realise was that it wasn't to spend my life with him, it was to teach me more about myself and the kind of men I had allowed into my world. It was to show me that I was capable of attracting a man, and I was worth something to someone. Victory did have someone in mind, but I first had to sort out some issues and realise that men like Jed are not right for me. He is a nice enough guy, but he knew he was good looking, and he knew I liked him, so he manipulated me, strung me along but offered me nothing.

Which now brings me to January 2016. Sixteen, my favourite number, something is going to change this year. Victory is going to reign. Stefan, my best friend, decided he was tired of me being single and all my moaning and groaning about how I was never going to meet anyone, so he decided to sign me up for online dating. Let the games begin. He first signed me up on a dodgy Christian site which wasn't a Christian site at all. I couldn't understand why I had so many guys messaging me, I had clearly stated my Christian beliefs, but they just seemed to ignore that. I found out later that you did not actually tell the truth on these sites. That makes zero sense to me!

Through this site I met Brett, who was a couple of years younger than me and had a seven-year-old daughter. We chatted for a bit, and he seemed super lovely. After a week we met for dinner. I was nervous but excited, while Harmony was worried sick. After dinner we went for a walk along the promenade, and he kissed me on the cheek goodnight - a lovely first date. We went on a second date a week later, which all went well, and we made plans to see each other on Australia Day. Then Sinister turned up. Brett just disappeared, refused to answer my messages or my phone calls, just total silence. It was the most bizarre thing. No explanation, nothing. I was not used to this online dating thing; I could not understand the lack of communication. We are not teenagers. It was then explained to me that this was a very common occurrence, and it had a name: "ghosting". A whole new world was opening to me.

After a couple of weeks, Stefan encouraged me to get back online but maybe with a more suitable dating site. I chose RSVP. I chatted with a few guys, but they were not suitable. One would say in his profile that he was a non-smoker, but when asked admitted that he did smoke - but not more than ten a day. Another just wanted a one-night stand, and I said "You did read my profile, right? I clearly stated I was a Christian and wanted a committed relationship." He did not understand my problem. I also had many younger men looking for a hook up, who were younger than my daughters. What is wrong with people? This online dating is a whole lot of crazy.

At the end of February, I met Ned, an Ecuadorian. We seemed to get on well and did lots of chatting. He sounded harmless so I agreed to meet him in the city. This was not a good date. Firstly, he was half an hour late, next he lied about his height. He was a lot shorter than me, and he kept going on about how tall I was. I said my profile listed my height on it, and he said, "But everyone lies on their profile!" Not me. He then had no plans for the afternoon, but eventually decided to take me to a Spanish restaurant. Good idea. After traipsing through the city trying to find it, we finally sat down for a late lunch. He ordered us paella. Yum. He asked if I wanted a drink, I told him no thank you and that I was happy with water. He told me to get up and get my own water, and while I was at it, to get him one. He finished his and then asked me to go get him another. Such a gentleman. He was very much into the idea that women are to cook, clean and look after children. This was not going well. After lunch we sat in Hyde Park for a couple of hours. I wanted to escape but he was captivated by me. I decided I would share my faith as a way to deter him, but he loved hearing about God and what I believed in. He couldn't wait to come to church with me. I even told him he did not need a girlfriend; he needed a saviour. Eventually I managed to escape. We were not compatible, but he had never met anyone like me, and he was keen to pursue this. I wrote him a story explaining how we were not meant to be.

Finally, we get to the good bit. I had been stalking a guy on RSVP for a few days. When you view someone's profile, they can see that you have looked. It is how I knew a few men had been consistently looking at mine, but they had not messaged me. If you wanted to send someone a message it cost money, however it was free to send someone a "kiss" letting them know you are interested. Well, I did not want to spend money and I wanted this guy to take the initiative and send me a message. I had to convince him I was interested, so looking at his profile daily made it obvious. Finally, he sent me a message. It was adorable. He had noticed I had been looking, but he wasn't sure why. He said he was concerned because he lived in a less fancy suburb than me and was only a blue-collar worker. I messaged back that although he was a bit far away, we could work it out. I also let him know that I was not a snob, and my best friend was a tradie. I was not looking for someone with multiple degrees who worked in an office block in the city, I needed a good honest person, who knew how to work hard and pay his taxes. A good strong Christian man. I had hit the jackpot. We messaged each other on RSVP for a week and finally on the Friday I asked for his mobile number so I could text him, as he was going camping for the weekend with mates and would be without internet and limited mobile reception. I spent the weekend sending him tons of texts asking all sorts of random questions. We then agreed to chat on the phone on Sunday night after church. Scary stuff. He rang and we spoke for over two hours, until his phone died. What I did not know at the time was this was very late for him, as he gets up at 5am to start work, and he was so nervous that he walked the block while we talked. That is over two hours of walking, people must have thought he was casing the place. He said he had never spoken to anyone for this long. He found talking to me easy, and he could not believe how much information I managed to pull out of him. I had been so worried about what his voice would sound like, as I do not like strong Australian accents or someone who mumbles. As it turned out his voice was perfect - a bit of England, New Zealand and Australia all rolled into one; clear, strong, and deep. I was hooked.

Not much sleep was had by me that night. "Lord, is this the one you have chosen for me? Do not let my heart be broken again. I want Your best for me. I pray Hunter is the one." We texted each other on Monday and he asked if he could come over as he could not wait another second to meet me. We decided to meet at my favourite local restaurant. I raced home from work, dressed in a pretty yellow dress, high heels, and make-up. That is big for me. I did not want to mess this up as I knew he was ticking all the boxes. When I arrived, he was waiting for me. Now I had to eat, stay calm and have a meaningful conversation. I only managed to eat half my risotto, I just kept looking at him. He was so handsome and so nice. The restaurant became very noisy, so we left. Hunter wanted to go for a walk but not in these heels, so I asked him back to my place. Very forward of me but I knew my boarders were home, and we wouldn't be alone. We had a cup of tea and chatted about all sorts of things, there was never an awkward moment. We just seemed to understand each other and were very similar in a lot of ways. I walked him out to his car, and he held my hands and just looked at me. He then kissed me on the forehead and drove away. It was lovely. A very successful first date. Victory.

Chapter 16

MY NEW BEAU

I COULD NOT believe after 13 years of being on my own that I had actually found a sweet, kind, funny, strong and honest man. A man who loved the Lord. He was an answer to my prayers. We both felt from that very first moment a peace and a confidence that we were destined to meet. I now believed in love at first sight. The Friday after our first date I drove to Hunter's house. here is my diary entry.

18 March, 2016

I left work at 2.30pm so I would not stress about driving through peak hour traffic, you see today I have come to Hunter's home. The drive over was uneventful, which I am grateful for. And surprise,

surprise, I found his house without a problem. Lucky it was easy, unlike finding my home. I am feeling very brave walking into his home when I have only met him once. He was still at work, so he told me to go in through the back door. Most people would call me stupid. Oh well, we all know what I am like, crazy. I made myself comfortable on the lounge and had literally just opened my book when Hunter comes home. Now I am nervous. He is feeling confident because he is in his environment, while I am freaked out. Stomach churning, butterflies careening, head spinning moment. Awkward but so worth it. I need to be brave. Override the fear with Victory boldness. You can do this. He has had to go to a meeting, so I am just sitting here reading my book. I am quite comfortable here until he returns. Which is now time for that confidence to kick in. Nope not happening. Oh well, let's just see what happens. All good, I pray. Why do we always have to eat on dates? Such an effort. I am only writing to keep myself calm. Let's just have fun and see where this goes.

A week later was Easter and it was time for Hunter to meet my family: Harmony and Mitchell and my parents. I was so excited and could not wait for them to meet him. Of course, they all loved him, why wouldn't they? Harmony gave him a letter; I have no idea what was written but I am sure it was "Look after my mum or else". He took it very graciously and even sent her one back. The following day it was my turn to go four-wheel-driving with his friends. Hunter started making such a racket in the kitchen at 6am, preparing lunch and breakfast smoothies. He thought I was highly entertaining, witnessing what I am like pre coffee. I think I managed to thank him for the smoothie, I'm not sure if I communicated well. It really is impossible to do so without coffee, especially at the crack of dawn. We had a delightful day driving through the bush and spending time with his friends. I was falling hard for this man.

Over the next few months, we each got to know each other's family and friends. I was well liked by his friends and all my family and friends loved him. Everyone was so happy for us. Hunter has five grown-up children, four boys and one girl. It was a lot of people for me to get to know. I found it a struggle getting to know them - I felt they did not want to let me in. Hunter, even though separated from his first wife for many years, had not actually divorced - and now that we were dating it really needed to be sorted out. I felt the boys were a little resentful towards me and they all stood by their mother's decision to take Hunter to the cleaners in a brutal settlement. Put it this way: there was an underlying tension between the boys and myself. Victory really needed to help me break down the barriers and help me to learn to understand these adult children.

04 April, 2016

It hasn't even been a month and yet I feel so connected to one incredible individual. You see I am the one that believed I was not supposed to find someone to love and be loved by. After years of praying and trusting and believing and crying out to the Lord for Victory I had actually given up. But

God placed a fighting spirit within me and I chose to rise up and believe, to go on the search. Interesting how I have always managed to start businesses, but not find a boyfriend. Well, all that changed. I prayed and searched and prayed. When God answers prayers He does so with precision. He doesn't just give you a small amount of what you ask and believe for, He gives you over and above all that you believe for. He sees me and knows me and provides what is good and right just for me. I praise God for the determination He placed within me to search the internet just one more time and I thank Him that one Hunter Simpson had the spare stamps on RSVP to send me a message.

I realise that all fairy tales have challenges, but when Victory is with you in a relationship, these challenges can be faced together and brought under His authority. I understand that I am living in a bubble of happiness, and reality might be just around the corner, but I am going to enjoy all the moments ahead. The fun, the good, the naughty, the hard, the time, the distance, the laughter, the tears, the frustration, the joy. I will enjoy the journey to the fullest.

This man can turn my belly into jelly and set my heart racing, but what I like most is seeing him with his arms raised high in church, giving God the glory.

The toughest part of this relationship was the distance we lived away from each other. Without traffic it would take an hour to reach each other's homes. I know we were only new, but I wanted to spend as much time as possible with him. The early stages of any relationship are so magical. One day Hunter just happened to pop into my office for a coffee and ended up coming over to Harmony's place for dinner. He left from there to go back to his place. When I finally arrived home from Harmony's, I discovered that he had stopped at my place and replaced the window in my dining room that the kookaburra had smashed. I felt so loved and cared for. Is this actually happening to me? Someone who truly cares for me and my needs.

During the month of May we were off to the Gold Coast for Hunter's dads 80th birthday. Time to meet his parents and siblings, who lived in New Zealand and would be over here for the party. Hunter thought it would be amusing to tell me that his younger brother had served time in prison for hitting a guy in the local hardware store. I believed it, but it was not true. He loved paying out on me, he had a cheeky sense of humour, which of course I loved. We had a lovely weekend with most of his extended family. I clicked with them all. They were a very loving and caring family who accepted me and loved seeing Hunter so happy.

12 July, 2016: A text message I sent to Hunter.

Before we were dating, I would often go to my daughters for dinner. It helped break up my week and it was a free meal. We would watch our TV series and then I would drive home, which is only 10 minutes away. The problem was I would on so many occasions cry my way home. Cry tears and cry out to God. I was so incredibly lonely, but no one knew that because I was very good at putting on a brave face and very good at keeping busy but driving home to my empty house was sometimes so overwhelming. I really did not want to live life alone anymore, so the tears would pour down my face and I would arrive home so utterly sad.

Tonight, I left Harmony's, and the tears came back. This time they were not for me. God heard my cry and answered my prayers. He has given me the man I had been believing for and I am so incredibly happy. The tears are of joy, but I also cannot help but cry for all the people I know and all the ones I do not know, who have not been blessed as I have, and I pray they too can find someone to love and be loved by. My heart breaks for them because I know how hard it is to go it alone. Thank you for being the one God has blessed me with. You are everything I have ever prayed for and so, so much more.

Throughout our first year of dating, we spend many hours sitting in his back yard chatting about us, about life, about where we were headed, about what we wanted from each other, and where we would live. Our communication was open and honest, we made sure we discussed everything. It was a firm foundation for our future together. Our biggest concern was where we would live, as we both had our own businesses. We had to believe that we would be able to come up with a solution that suited both of us. So long as we kept talking, we would work out all the nuances of our relationship.

The first step was settlement and divorce for

Hunter. It became very unpleasant and caused him a lot of stress. There were times when he became very disheartened, and he struggled to stay positive. Eventually the settlement went through, and she did very well out of it. Hunter was not happy with the result, but we were both relieved it was over and we could put it all behind us.

In August we went on our first holiday together. I had won a trip to Krabi, Thailand. We had so much fun. He was a great travelling companion, easy-going, and he loved to explore. Perfect for me, as being a travel consultant, I wanted to see everything. We hired a scooter and rode around to see all the sights. We walked along the beach outside our resort and found a quaint hut restaurant where we drank pina coladas and ate delicious Thai food. The memories of this trip will always raise a smile. I was the happiest person alive.

At Christmas time we went with Hunter's tradition of camping. All my family and friends thought this was hilarious as they all knew I camped well at the Sheraton or Hilton, but not so well under canvas. The things we do for love. I would have you know, I really enjoyed it. We went with other church families, so I was able to get to know them a little better. Hunter was a camp expert. He had everything set up, including a kitchen sink. I was even allowed to take Nessie, my coffee machine. It really was glamping, but I could say to everyone I went camping for Christmas. If it weren't for the out-of-control mosquitoes it would have been close to perfect. I looked forward to Christmas the following year; I liked this new tradition. Our children were all welcome to join us if they so desired.

Hunter proposed to me 14 March 2017, exactly one year from our first date. He totally tricked me, making out that this date was no big deal, telling me to book a table at the same restaurant. He said we'd just go have dinner. I was not impressed. But when dinner was over, he gave me a frog-prince charm for my pandora bracelet, and said it was him. We then jumped into the car, and he put on his favourite love songs and drove us to Warriewood Beach headlands. Harmony and Hunter had set up all these fairy lights and white roses with a light sign, saying "Will you marry me?" He got down on his knee and asked me to marry him. I believe I squealed. Harmony and Mitchell then jumped out of the bush and Melody was on their phone. It was very romantic.

It turns out that Hunter had asked the girls back in November if he could marry me. He gave both the girls an angel charm saying he was letting them hand over the care of me into his hands. They both cried. They all went to the jewellery shop together to pick my ring, which I absolutely love. They all had to keep this a secret until March and in that time, I was constantly complaining that he had not proposed yet.

We decided to be married on August 19th, and had already booked a trip to Turkey, so we could turn that into our honeymoon. We were married at Palm Beach Golf course, where my cousin worked. We were married out on the green overlooking Lion Island. Supposedly it was cold, but I didn't notice. The girls and I arrived in golf buggies, they were dressed in white with boots, and I was dressed in this crazy, pale pink wedding dress. No one was surprised as they all knew pink was my colour. The wedding party walked up to the lighthouse for photos but unfortunately half of them ended up having asthma attacks. My best friend, Stefan, who started me off on my online dating journey, was a groomsman - but he had to abort the photo session and go in search of Ventolin. The photos were amazing however, it was well worth the climb.

It was a fantastic day, and I was very blessed with just how much other people contributed to this day. They were all so happy for us that they showed their appreciation by their generosity. Harmony and Mitchell paid for the photographer and Harmony made the cake, it looked amazing and tasted delicious. Stefan paid for the flowers and the Kombi vans that brought us to the wedding. My florist friend made up all the bouquets for nothing, and paid for the flowers in mine, and they were spectacular. My cousin managed to get a discount for the venue as she worked there. Jayden paid for the invitations, and they were magnificent. I was also able to arrange it so that my travel agency paid for the honeymoon. We were truly blessed, and without all this help we would not have had such an incredible day. I was so excited about all that Victory was doing and going to do for this marriage.

Hunter loved Turkey; it was his first time experiencing the Middle East. We spent the first five nights in a little town a couple hours from Istanbul on the Black Sea. We enjoyed all the different foods, especially the breakfasts. Hunter struggled with jet lag, but that wasn't an issue as we had nowhere to be. We then joined a tour with four other travel consultants. Hunter enjoyed all the information our guide shared and all the sites we experienced. The sights and sounds of Istanbul, walking over ancient ruins, hot air ballooning in Cappadocia, the ruins of

Ephesus, and he was also honoured to go to Gallipoli and show our respects to our fallen soldiers.

Our marriage was off to an incredible start, and I could not wait to see all that Victory had planned for us.

Chapter 17

FIRST YEAR OF MARRIAGE

THE FIRST YEAR of marriage was absolute bliss. Because of the travel required for work, for part of the time during the week we stayed in separate houses - but we managed to make it work. I would drive over to his place on a Friday afternoon and then drive back on Monday morning in time for work. Hunter would come over a couple of nights during the week. Many people thought this arrangement was perfect for a marriage, but we found the separation hard, like many couples we really wanted to see each other every day. We attended Hunter's church, which I still attend today, and I was starting to make new friends and settle into the life of being a wife again. I have to say,

I love being a wife. I was in a place of contentment and happiness for the first time in forever.

Of course, we really wanted to live in one place, so we started real estate searching for a home in my area. It seemed to be the best solution as I had an actual office while Hunter travelled to his places of work. Houses were triple the price of those in Hunter's suburb, though, so we could not buy a property on our own. Hunter got along famously with Harmony and Mitchell, and they had the incomes to allow us to borrow more, so we looked at properties that were or could be converted into dual occupancy, similar to my current home. We did discuss buying my parents out of my place, but it wasn't very suitable for Hunter's needs. He really needed a garage or storage space for all his work equipment, plus he was concerned that my place was going to need massive repairs in a couple of years. We had a look at a few properties and even put offers in, but they always sold for a little more than we could afford.

So, Hunter and I decided to start looking in his suburb where we could afford to buy by ourselves. His current place, which we aptly named the Love Shack, was cute - but we both wanted something we owned together. While staying at the Love Shack one weekend Hunter had just laid some turf down out the front; he loved a fancy lawn. During the night some people stole it - they had rolled it up and taken it! I could not believe it, who even does that? Hunter replaced the stolen grass and yet again it got stolen. I was horrified, this just doesn't happen in my area - I never even locked my car. When Hunter replaced it for a third time, we spray painted it pink. This time we managed to keep the grass! The Love Shack was also broken into once when we were away at Christmas time, camping. It was time to find a home away from this busy street, where there were too many opportunities for the locals to help themselves.

The more work needed on the place; the more Hunter wanted it. Hunter has an amazing talent for renovating, the houses he has renovated have been transformed from total disasters to masterpieces. He is a clever and talented man. We looked at one house where Hunter thought "no way", but I thought, "it is quirky, perfect". After going to an auction for a simple cottage that we could have easily restored, but losing out to a higher bidder, my mind kept coming back to the quirky house that overlooked a park and a golf course. The interesting thing is when we looked at it, I felt terribly ill. There was something not right about the place, and I actually had to sit down so I wouldn't vomit. Despite this feeling of dread, I still really liked this house. I could see the potential and the charm of it. It also had massive storage under the house, perfect for Hunter's requirements. We placed an offer, and we purchased our first home together. We still had the issue of working in different areas far apart, and I still had to own my place because my parents lived with me and owned a portion of that house, but it was great to finally own something together. It was a project we could do as a team and turn into something magical. A place where people would walk in and feel instantly at ease and marvel at our creative geniuses. It would combine Hunter's skills, and my flare for the dramatic, toned down of course, or Hunter would have had a fit. Over the next couple of years this house was transformed. Hunter knocked down walls and opened the lounge room and dining room. The massive sandstone fireplace that dominated the small room was removed and we put in a modern fire which was see-through from both sides. We installed a beautiful barn door made using the old panelling from the dining room walls, painted in lime wash blue. I would come up with an idea and Hunter made it happen. Hunter had only ever designed his homes to be neutral, plain, and simple, as it appealed to many and did not require much creative thought. I love being bold in design and colour but tried not to overwhelm him with too many crazy ideas. Hunter put in an ensuite, and I chose tiles featuring the names of cities and places, very apt for a travel consultant. He let me loose on the main bathroom and I transformed it into a kaleidoscope of colour, using different tiles, giving it a mosaic feel. The tiler had a lot of fun doing the job. Hunter did not know what to do with the hallway cupboard, so I suggested a wet room, so that when you opened it there were hooks for coats and shelves for boots. He even placed power points in there so he could charge up his tools. It was such a joy coming home on a Friday night and seeing what he had accomplished that week. It was always such a pleasant surprise. I was excited about all our future homes and just what we could do to transform them together. Victory was in this perfect match, Hunter could create anything we desired, and I could design anything, within reason.

Hunter and I had very different backgrounds. I was the girl from the beaches and lived a very sheltered life. I travelled the world and saw much poverty and destruction in the places I visited, but I always came home to my very protected suburb. Hunter lived in rougher areas and as a young man he was a sheep shearer. He travelled throughout New Zealand and Western Australia as a shearer and mingled with some pretty tough men. I was a Christian from the age of 15 while he became a Christian in his late 30s. We were chalk and cheese, but we did not care, we were in love and complimented each other in our differences. My entire family, including my extended family, do not swear - it is just something we never got into the habit of doing. Hunter and his boys, like everyone else on the planet, did. Hunter liked the idea of not swearing around me, he thought it made him think before speaking and helped temper his anger about something. I appreciated the effort and understood that while he was at work, he no doubt relaxed in the way he spoke. I look back now and feel I manipulated him with this, which was not my intention, I just think it is good for us to have some self-control when it comes to our language. When the time came for grand babies, we certainly would not be swearing around them, and when speaking to our parents we didn't use colourful language. It was easy for me as I never picked up the habit, but I realise it would have been hard for Hunter to watch his mouth. I think my point is, when you merge your life with another, there are certain compromises that need to happen, especially when you are older and have set ways of doing things. Hunter never did, and never will, put the toilet seat down, he does not see why he should. I do not like the look of the seat up, it makes the bathroom look cheap - however, why argue over a toilet seat? Hunter was an early riser, and I was not. He would generally go to bed before me, and this sometimes hurt as I wanted to stay up late with him on the weekends, but he was unable to keep his eyes open. I love to read, and he loves Sudoku. He only watched very violent movies;

Disney was not allowed. I learnt to watch them with him. I did not mind them as it meant I was spending time with him. I still cannot believe he has never seen the Sound of Music. I was all about colour, whereas he liked things subdued. Hunter loved going to see bands and I loved the theatre. We saw Ice House, James Taylor, Foreigner, and we sat in the audience to *Beautiful*, *The Bodyguard*, *Finding Neverland* and *Jersey Boys*. We opened each other's eyes to new and exciting things. We were both in the wonder of each other. Sinister, however, was hovering close by.

During our first few years we attended many family weddings. Two of Hunter's sons were married, as well as his sister, and my nieces. We travelled to Oberon, Wellington, and Melbourne for these events. Everyone was so happy seeing us together, doing life.

In February of 2018 I turned 50, yikes. We decided on no party as we had just had our wedding party six months before. Instead, Hunter and I just went on a three-day comedy cruise. It was a lot of fun, we enjoyed the jazz bar and often stayed listening to the live music until late. On my actual birthday, while we were munching our way through breakfast sailing the seas, Hunter showed me a photo of a pinball machine. He knew I had a secret desire to own one. I said that was cool but then I realised it was in our home. He had actually bought me a pinball machine for my birthday! I could not believe it. Ralph only ever bought me presents for the house, but this beautiful man gave me a present that was just for me. I could not wait to go home and play. Best surprise ever.

Hunter was always putting himself down, saying how he did not do well buying gifts. He did so much better than he realised. He might not always have known what to buy someone for a birthday, but he was always generous when there was no pressure. Every fortnight since we started dating, he would have a rose delivered to my office. It was his way of saying I love you. Every morning he sent me a text with "good morning beautiful," and every time we walked somewhere together, he held my hand. These are the presents we all need, not the over-the-top materialistic things. Tangible, caring and loving acts of kindness. This man was my man. I was so blessed.

In this first year Hunter helped finance Harmony and Mitchell with their first apartment, and we half owned it with them. We found the worst possible one-bedder on the beaches. It was so bad that you gagged just walking through the place. It had years of old pizza boxes stacked high (and that was the best part), the owner was a smoker, so the walls were a grimy grey colour, and above where he sat were squashed bugs all over the wall. I cannot even put into words the bathroom; you could see where he leant up against the wall with his hand while he relieved himself. The toilet had never been cleaned. It was totally cringeworthy. When we went to have a second look at it, the owner was passed out on the lounge and there was no rousing him. Hunter thought it was perfect, the price was negotiated, and we had an apartment. After completely demolishing the interior, it was turned into a delightful apartment 200 meters from the beach. A couple of years later Harmony and Mitchell bought us out and they now have an investment that will only grow in value over time. This is just one example of Hunter's generosity - he provided the deposit needed, and the skills needed to renovate. The crazy thing is, the tiny one-bedroom unit is worth more than a house in the suburb Hunter and I had our home in. It is remarkable how real estate prices vary so drastically in my city.

In May of that year, I was offered a heavily discounted small ship cruise with Silversea. Only 120 people on a luxury vessel through the Solomon Islands and Vanuatu. Hunter and I experienced 10 days of total luxury. We even had a butler who delivered our lattes in the morning while we were still in bed. Hunter had never experienced anything like it. The best part was Hunter is an avid snorkeler and the reefs around this part of the world are next level. We visited the villages on the islands where the locals would perform traditional dances and sing about their culture. Hunter was in his element, playing with the village children, and after every performance he would seek out the village elder or chief and thank them for having us as their guests. He was so respectful of them and made the effort to show them how much he appreciated them allowing us to visit. He felt very uncomfortable hobnobbing with our fellow guests as they were all highly accomplished lawyers, pilots, bankers, and doctors, but not one of them showed any appreciation for the locals. Hunter outshone them all. It is not about your so-called achievements; it is about your kindness and respect. I was honoured to call him my husband and let everyone know he was an accomplished home renovator and handyman.

It was moments like these, however, that highlighted differences. I was never embarrassed by who he was, but I believe he was. I was comfortable around wealth; my clients spent a huge amount of money on holidays, but I did not let that determine the way I treated them. Money never came easily to me, I struggled to pay the mortgage every month, but we are all equal in my eyes, no matter how much we have in the bank or how big our homes are. Hunter often called me his "Beaches snob" to remind us always of our differences. I did the same by always referring to his town as Westie territory. I would often joke that I could wear my pyjamas with Ugg boots down to the local shops and I would look just like everyone else. My girls were privately educated and successful while his children were home schooled and struggled a bit to find their footing. It was a great divide that never concerned me, but I believe very much influenced Hunter. He wanted to fit into my world but did not know how. His answer was that I needed to fit into his world, but he did not know how to articulate this with me. He wanted the revelation to come to me, and for me to offer to move permanently into our home and commute to work. Commuting, however, would mean up to an hour and half each way for me and I was not prepared to do that. Looking back now, I should have been prepared to do anything, even close my business or work from home. Hindsight is always a beautiful thing.

Chapter 18

IT ALL FELL DOWN

THE SECOND YEAR of our marriage started off strong. We were ready to tackle another year living part of the time apart, but we would try to find a solution that worked for both of us so that we could be together. I was convinced that Victory had a plan. I was offered an amazing price on flights to New York, so with much harassment I convinced Hunter we should go. He had no interest in going to America, but I explained to him that travelling with a professional would make the trip outstanding. I also found us tickets to see Elton John and one of his favourite bands, Fleetwood Mac as both were performing at Madison Square Gardens. I wanted this trip to blow his mind, I wanted to make sure we did everything possible. We travelled in

March, so it was cold but not freezing, with a touch of snow on the ground. I booked eight nights at the Novotel on Times Square with a view - great location. Hunter struggles with jet lag but we did not have time for rest, so I dragged him out of bed every morning, as we had much to do and see. We experienced New York to the fullest - going to the top of the Rockefeller centre; taking in a graffiti tour of Brooklyn, a food tour of Little Italy and a walking tour of lower Manhattan to learn about slavery; strolling through Central Park; enjoying theatre nights; visiting famous restaurants and food trucks; climbing inside the Statue of Liberty; and seeing the 9/11 museum. We did not rest, and we had so much fun. After our eight nights we hired a car and drove to Pennsylvania and stayed in a delightful bed and breakfast, where the hosts arranged for us to have dinner with their Amish neighbours. It was a fantastic experience, seeing how they lived and how they ran their dairy farm. Hunter loved it as his family were dairy farmers. He fell in love with all the Amish handmade furniture, and I could just picture him in retirement with overalls on, making furniture to sell at markets. We then travelled to Washington DC and did a Segway tour of the capital's sights. Finally, we had our last couple of nights in Philadelphia, learning all about the history of this city and all things *Rocky*. We had an incredible time, the type of holiday I loved, especially when I could take someone who had never experienced anything like it. I wish I could press pause on my life at this very moment and not have to face what was to come.

We had only been home a couple of months when something happened that sent Victory to the curb and put Sinister in charge. I cannot really pinpoint what happened, it just did. Hunter suddenly turned sullen, he stopped holding my hand when we were out, he stopped sending me my "good morning, beautiful" text I had received every day, and the rose he sent to me every fortnight just ceased. I had no idea what I had done, or how to fix it.

20 May, 2019

I can't believe I am writing this, but you know me, I need to write. My marriage is in crisis, Hunter has checked out. He is just not showing up. He has put us in the friendship box. The intimacy has gone. It's like what we had no longer exists. I've tried talking to him but he is not interested. He tells me silly reasons for the rift, like not eating well, or living in two places, but they are just excuses. Our lives are good, and we have much to be thankful for. Yes, things can be inconvenient, but they're minor compared to the bond we had. He just does not care. He is not interested in fixing us. I am lost for what to do except pray, pray and pray.

I pushed and pushed for an answer, but I was continually getting stone walled. Finally, he opened his heart just a smidge. We need to take a step back to when we first met to explain this well. Hunter was a hunter. When I first met him, this was explained to me, and although I do not like the thought of any animal being shot, I understood he enjoyed it. Hunter had been to Africa just after he left his first wife and he had on display four larger-than-life trophy heads: kudu, springbok, warthog, and wildebeest. They were very domineering and confronting, however he had them displayed in a nook in the hallway, so they didn't dominate an entire room. I decided the best way to embrace these dead beasts was to make them my pets, so I gave them all names and patted them when I walked past. A few months after we started dating, they disappeared off the wall. I could not believe my eyes. I asked Hunter where they had gone, and his reply was that he did not need them anymore and had decided to give them to one of his sons. I took this to mean that Hunter knew I was not a fan, and he was so content in our relationship that he was willing to gift them to his son. How wrong was my assumption! It so happens that he gifted them to his son because he was afraid, he would lose them in his divorce settlement that was still being sorted out. He never wanted to lose them, and so by giving them to his son he could have them returned to him later. Anyway, now you have the background here is the smidge that Hunter opened up to me. He found out that his son had sold them, and for very little money. He was so devastated that he plunged into a deep depression. He could not believe that he had lost his trophy heads, they represented an incredible time of his life, and even though I would never understand it, they brought him much joy. Hunter loves his sons with his all, so he was very quick to forgive. Which is the way Victory would want it. The issue was, and now I am only guessing, his ex-wife was the reason all this happened, and I suspect that forgiving her was a whole different story. I believe Sinister jumped right into his heart and set up camp. Not forgiving someone even when they do not deserve forgiveness, is a trap that is very hard to climb out of. I don't even think Hunter realised this is what happened. He did struggle with forgiving her when we first met, but he had worked through this. The problem is, Sinister just does not quit, and when given an opportunity, he takes a hold. If we don't spend time examining our hearts and making sure we are free from strongholds like unforgiveness, they can take root. Now I am only speculating here, but it is a logical explanation for his behaviour. When he talked to me about It, he said he was heartbroken that this had happened to the point that it took him weeks to share it with me and allowed himself to slip into depression. He tracked down the heads in the end and found them for sale in a local gun shop. We organised to buy them back for a lot more than they were sold for. Hunter did not care how much it cost him, he had them back.

I was hoping that now the trophy heads were back in his possession his depression would improve and our relationship would start to get back to where it was before all this happened. I must admit that I did not understand depression. I had been through a lot in my life, but I never felt like I could not go on, or function. I turned to God and sought Victory when things were tough. Hunter had struggled with depression a few times throughout his life and although he denied he was depressed, I felt like this was depression to some degree. He never came out of this funk. It took him down, which is why I think it was not only depression but something more Sinister. I did not want these animals displayed in our beautiful home, but he wanted to see them and appreciate them. He put them in the back room, but you could see this room as soon as you entered our home. It detracted from everything else in the house. The way I describe it is if I had insisted that we have a florescent pink lounge, front and centre, so that was all anyone would see, and it would dominate any space. What was happening was, people who used to come around and admire our renovations and our home, now only saw dead animals. They dominated every conversation. I wanted people to admire our home, but Hunter wanted people to admire his hunting skills. Maybe I should have just let it go, after all I loved Hunter with all my heart. Eventually he put them in the study, but he was not happy with that. I tried to encourage him to turn one of our spare rooms into a den or create something downstairs, but no, he wanted them in the back room for all to see.

By this time, we barely functioned as a couple. I would go over there on weekends, but he only came to my place one day a week now, he said it was all too hard. He started to dislike Harmony, even though they had always had a great relationship. Harmony can be bossy and want her way, but her strengths are far greater than her weaknesses. I tried to make sure I did not put her needs and wants above Hunter's so he could see that he was number one in my life, but he did not care. Our marriage was at a standstill.

In August we had a family gathering for Hunter's parents in the Cook Islands. I organised everything and what a job that was. We were a rowdy lot; the other guests were not impressed with the young adults staying up to the early hours of the morning making a racket. I love his family and really enjoy spending time with them. There were a few technical difficulties throughout the week, but I was able to sort them out. Hunter's parents were so grateful that I was there to help sort out everything. I was very much appreciated by the entire family. It was a lot of fun and great to spend time with Hunter and his family. As well as this trip we also did a couple of weekend camping trips. I really enjoyed camping now but that was because

Hunter was such a capable camper. These weekends were special, and we were able to have deeper conversations, but when we arrived back home Hunter would continue to ignore me.

8 November, 2019

Stop and pray. I want to voice my opinion. I want to hurt him like he is hurting me. I want to fix it but at the same time run from it. The pain is great but not greater than God. He knows how hard this is for me. I don't understand why Hunter does not want to fix whatever is getting to him. I don't understand mental illness. I get sad and I run to God. I take my stuff to Him constantly and cry out with all I have, so I don't understand why Hunter doesn't do that. Why isn't he crying out, on his knees trying to sort through his issues? Why bury his head in the sand and pretend all is well? Nothing's well, it's terrible. I want to say so much to him, but I know that is not a good idea. I need to pray, not blurt. I need to be gracious and understanding, not brutal. Now is not the time for honesty and accountability, it's just time to shut up and pray and love. Victory, help me to stay shut up, don't let me open my mouth because what will come out could damage the fragile state Hunter is in. Lord, give me keys and wisdom on what to do and what to say. Should I send him words of encouragement, or is that just going to make him feel worse about himself? God, minister to him, show him your loving kindness, but also teach him how to pray and how to reach out to You in his desperate need. Show him you see and hear him, and You are the place he needs to go to. He needs to hand his hurts, concerns and difficulties over to You. He needs scripture to mediate on so he fills his mind with goodness. Turn his thoughts to You Lord. Help me to love and be quiet, but when it is time to love and talk, that it is with your wisdom.

A couple of weeks after I wrote this, I was off to Hawaii with three friends. I wanted to take people away to experience one of my favourite destinations. Again, I get so much enjoyment showing others worldwide destinations. We had a crazy fun week, with lots of sightseeing, shopping in the Thanksgiving, and Black Friday sales, and lots of eating. Hawaii is a great place to go as it has so much to offer and the best climate. We hired a mini convertible and zoomed around the island of Oahu, we climbed Diamond Head and nearly collapsed from exhaustion, we even hired push bikes and cycled around Waikiki. It was great to have a break from all the chaos of home.

26 November, 2019

I'm sitting here in Waikiki enjoying my week with the girls but feeling like my life is about to fall apart. I'm trying to hold the tears back because I am here to have fun, but I am feeling sick to my stomach. I'm not sure I have a marriage to go home to. Hunter has become so obsessed with dead animals and he knows how much I hate it. It's like he is deliberately baiting me trying to get me to say it is over. Unfortunately, it reminds me of how Ralph used to say and do things to deliberately force me to react. To force me to have the guts to leave him so he could say I left him. I feel this is what Hunter's trying to get me to do: actually say "I can't live with all this dead animal stuff so I'm leaving you". I really feel that is what he wants. God is this the actual truth? Is his shooting etc more important than his marriage? I'm feeling so stuck right now. I can't do anything because I am on the other side of the world. He just told me he is picking up a skin. I've always told him that I could never have a skin in the house. So now I have 5 dead heads, 2 antlers and a deer skin. It's my worst nightmare. I'm so confused. I thought he understood this about me and was willing to just shoot not display, but ever since he got Facebook with all its shooting groups he's gotten out of control. I don't know if he is testing me like Ralph use to. "Will you still love me if I display all this or are you going to walk?" It throws me back to when Ralph told me he couldn't have kids. "Will you stay with me?" If I'm being truthful, I'm not sure. God am I just supposed to accept this.? It's like I have no say. My opinion doesn't matter, he's the boss. Oh Lord, I have been here before. I don't want this. I want a husband that will give up the world for me. That is so in love with me that I'm worth the sacrifice. Is this what he wants from me? For me to say "I love you so much I'll let you hang dead stuff everywhere"? Can I do that? Am I wrong wanting a house that we can both enjoy? Does he really want out of this marriage? Because if he does, then he just has to say so. I don't want to play silly games again. If he doesn't love me then just tell me. If he's doing this to test me then that is unacceptable. I will not be manipulated again. I think he thinks I am manipulating him because I won't allow these things in our home, but he knew this from the first month we were together. I never kept my feelings about this from him, but he kept them from me.

Not only is there a problem with the animals, but he is also keeping secrets from me - but he is constantly exposed. Hence why you shouldn't keep secrets from your spouse. Secrets always come out. He doesn't talk to me about issues, he doesn't share his heart, he doesn't desire me. I feel I have become a total inconvenience and he is doing his level best to push me away. It's like he is trying to give me an ultimatum- if you don't allow the animals then you don't want me and you need to leave.

So now I have to try to enjoy the rest of the week knowing that there is a possibility that I'm going home to a distressed marriage. I honestly just want to ring him and have it out, but I know I'll be the one doing all the talking and he will just be silent. I'll have no idea what he is thinking or feeling but he will know exactly what I am thinking and hate me for it. Somehow it will all be my fault things are this bad, after all he was always a hunter and I knew this before marriage, and so I should accept that this gives him the privilege of displaying his spoils regardless of my feelings.

God, I really need your help.

We struggled through the next six months, spending the Christmas break with one of his sons, then with Melody and Ken. There were some lovely moments where we seemed to be coming out from under Sinister, but there was an underlying tension that never went away. Call me naive but I truly believed we would eventually sort it out and Victory would once again reign in our marriage.

Chapter 19

WHAT EVEN?

WE HAD PLANNED a trip to New Zealand in March for a family wedding of Hunter's. I had booked great airfares six months before, and I had planned this incredible itinerary for after the family gathering. As per usual we had a great time with his family, with lots of laughs and a beautiful wedding. We then had 10 days of travelling around the top of the South Island, and I had planned the most romantic places possible. A "Purepod" was first on the agenda, we had to walk over a hill and arrive at this all-glass room overlooking a valley. It was magic. We then experienced quaint bed and breakfasts, an eco-lodge with a spa on our balcony, and a remote lodge with a renowned chef. I believed we were having a great time together, but

Hunter had times of sullenness. I ignored this and enjoyed the trip; we even swam with seals. Unbeknownst to me, Sinister had an evil plan that was about to be launched at me.

01 April, 2020

Wow, what a massive three weeks. I had no clue what was going to be before me as I travelled around New Zealand. I was doing what I love, travelling and spending precious time with my husband. I was enjoying myself, but little did I know the man travelling with me was about to pull the rug from beneath me. He was about to change my life drastically as was the Coronavirus. I sit here three weeks later thinking, "I had no idea". No clue as to what Sinister was going to attempt to do to stop me from moving forward. Despite all this mess, God reigns supreme; like Job in the Bible, Sinister can throw everything at me, but God has me in the palm of His hand. I will stand my ground, dig deep, worship my God, surrender control, hold onto the altar and never lose sight of who is in charge. I have to constantly stop, write, and remember the promises and favour of God. And that's okay for me to do. Whatever it takes to help me through this. As long as I continue to turn my eyes towards my living saviour I will come out on top. I will see Victory. He never lets us down.

Let's go back three weeks. After arriving home, Hunter went back to our joint home, and I went back to a business that was on the verge of collapse. Coronavirus had taken control of the world and slowly over the three weeks, one after the other of my bookings had to be cancelled. Travel is banned, my industry is currently no more. Unlike other businesses, we could not just shut up shop and walk away. I had to comfort and assist all my clients. I had to get them home, organise their refunds and console them about their trips that had been planned for months. It was exhausting, devastating, and mentally tough. I had to put my feelings to one side and give them my time and energy.

My travel agency, the business God and I built together, the dream and vision God birthed in me, the place I called my ministry, the clients I love and share life with, had all turned to dust. Sixteen years and now I had to lay it down. There was nothing that could be done at the time except hold my head high and know God and I loved doing this together. All the challenges, all the triumphs and all the incredible places we have travelled together. What a journey. What a joy. What a life. Now do not get me wrong, I had not closed down completely, I just did not have the income to keep trading. "But God". I was believing that I could put my travel agency in hiatus and then resurrect it from the ashes once the virus had stopped.

My clients were so supportive, and I knew they would be back to book, I just had to lean on God and ask Him for creative ways to keep my business open. How and where would I get income? Did I have to shut the office and work from home? Should I sell my home? These questions had to be meditated on and decisions made slowly. If I could keep the doors open, I thought, all that had been taken could be restored. God's favour and Victory would reign.

Now I must write about my marriage. This is so

much harder to talk about. Tears just track down my face as I write this. My husband decided he needed a break. He didn't contact me during this time when my business was sent down the plughole. He checked out, he couldn't deal with my pain and my chaos, so he just stopped communicating. Instead of being my rock, he decided he was not interested. He spent time with his boys, pretending all was good, while his wife cried and screamed into the air. Where was he? How could he desert me? Why wasn't he holding me tight assuring me that everything was going to be ok? Gone, gone, gone. Nothing. Not a word. Silence. It blows my mind. What sort of person does this and thinks it's ok? I cannot even treat my enemy like this, but he can treat his wife like this. I understand he is weak and can't handle things, but really? You can just push aside the one you vowed to be there for in everything? Gone, gone, gone. And his excuses were unacceptable, truly weak.

Excuse one: our holidays are too extravagant, and we live beyond our means.

Excuse two: I do not want to live with you, and I do not want to leave my local area.

Excuse three: I do not want to leave our church.

Excuse four: You do not take retirement seriously.

These were just ridiculous and each one of them could be resolved with communication and compromise.

I wrestled deeply with God in this time:

Where do I go from here? I know I am the strong one, I am the one that can and does cry out at the gates of heaven for help. I am the one who has the faith to know God has us in the palm of His hands and He will not let us go. He can bring us through all adversity and Victory is ours. Why can't Hunter see this? Where is his faith? I want to slap him, I want to question his faith, I just want to ask him where is his compassion? Who leaves his wife in the midst of calamity?

Enough, I have said enough. What I do know is I am going to be the one that forgives him. Who accepts him back just as he is. The one who is willing to make compromises to ensure this marriage works. I have to lay it all down, my dreams, my plans, my hopes. Throw it all down so my marriage lives. Can I do this? Of course, God gives me the Victory to do so. I married Hunter for life, through good and bad. Nothing except you, Lord, comes before my marriage. I signed the binding agreement, the covenant of a marriage. It is what I need to do, and I am not saying this is going to be a walk in the park, oh so far from it. It is going to take all that I have to make these changes. I might have to sell my house and live in our joint home, I might have to accept my business needs to close, no more overseas holidays, no more fancy clothes and new cars. All this might have to go for me to show Hunter it is all meaningless without him. He is my life; he is the commitment I made. My question to you Lord, is how do I do this and stay sweet, not let bitterness take a hold? I do not want to replace one set of issues with others, like resentment and regret. I have to willingly, lovingly lay these things down. If I have nothing, yet I have Hunter, that has to be enough. No greater love than he who lays his life down for his brother. Time for me to practice this. It is all just stuff. Love overrules all this.

I give all this over to you, Lord. You see my heart; you see my struggles. You know this is not easy for me, but what we do know is we cannot let Sinister win. He is cast out. He has no hold on my life, my marriage, my husband, my business, my health. I rest in you Lord. Show me wisdom on what steps I should take towards reconciliation. Holy Spirit, speak clearly to me so I take no wrong step. Keep me focused on You, not on me or any selfish gain I may desire. Only You God. Victory.

Footnote: I need to make note of all the mini miracles happening since this all started. Clients have bought me coffees, muffins, flowers, and wine. My local butcher gave me free meat, I received a balloon bouquet from Liz, so many messages of support from my community, free surgery that I needed, and cash from clients. Victory is letting me know all is well. We have got this.

After three weeks of silence and having to deal with my business, I made a desperate phone call to our church pastor, and I texted Hunter saying I believed we were worth fighting for. He eventually replied and I set up a meeting to see our pastor and his wife. I drove over to our home, but I had to stop at a park and sob my heart out. I rang a friend who prayed for me, and a lovely stranger came and knocked on my car window asking if I was okay. I needed to pull it together and ask Victory to have control. The meeting went well, there were a couple of items that came up that helped, but during the two hours nobody ever once used my name - I was either 'her', 'she' or 'wife'. I found this distracting and wanted to let them know my name. Hunter seemed to glean more from the session than I did. Our biggest battle was that we both tended to put our adult children before each other, and we had to discuss ways to not let this happen. We were advised to have communication dates and try to make it a friendly environment where Hunter could feel comfortable and open up.

Thanks to Covid I was able to move over to our home full time. I walked into our home on a Friday night and said, "I am here to stay." Hunter looked so happy because I had taken the initiative to move in and I had the faith to believe we could work it out. I made sure to fill Hunter's love tank to overflowing. Dinner cooked every night, encouraging text messages and post-its in his lunch. I tried to be loving and understanding - but unfortunately Hunter gave me nothing. He told me he no longer loved me, and I was now his best friend. Yes, you read that right, I had been placed in the friend zone after only two years of marriage. We took the advice of our pastor and had our communication dates, we discussed the things Hunter was worried about, and I felt our conversations went well, but they did not eventuate into any real change.

15 April, 2020

I am sitting here on my own late at night while Hunter went to bed at 7.50pm, and I am looking at our wedding photos displayed on the walls of our lounge room. There in the photos is a man that was so happy, so in love. Looking at me with so much joy. Where has he gone?

I spend my days in our home trying to stay upbeat, trying to stay committed, trying to look for the peace I keep singing about. Where did the "Morning, beautiful" go? Where did my rose disappear to? Whatever happened to my kiss goodbye and my kiss hello? It's just all gone. Now I have a husband that comes home and gives me a two minute run down of his day and then scrolls through Facebook until his dinner is served. As soon as he can he trots off to bed where he usually spends a bit more time on Facebook before turning off the light - ensuring he is asleep before I come to bed.

I'm not sure how much longer I can do this. I'm worn out, exhausted and just broken. I am giving myself completely to him. I am making sure I am cooking his dinner, asking if I can get him a drink, encourage him and be there for him. And I get nothing. I am not a selfish person and I have always enjoyed giving to others, but right now I am ready to be selfish. I do not want a loveless marriage. I do not want mediocre. I do not want to be empty of all joy, just to please the man I married.

Maybe it is time to admit defeat. Maybe I am not strong enough to push through. I need a lifeline. I need a glimmer of hope. Some small gesture to let me know he still cares.

One of our biggest pitfalls at this time was our living arrangements. He did not enjoy coming to my place during the week and he felt because we lived apart so much, it had caused irreparable damage. We discussed at length selling my home and finding somewhere to live that was a reasonable distance to commute for work for both of us. My friend's mother had recently passed away and her home would be coming on the market in the not-too-distant future. It was a perfect location, 30 minutes from my office and an easy 40-minute drive to Hunter's district, plus he could increase his work to incorporate the beaches area. I believed we both felt good about this possible scenario. If all went well, we could have found the perfect place to live together. This was not going to happen overnight, as we would have to renovate and sell my home. We also had to make sure my dad was on board as it meant he would also lose his home, and Harmony and Mitchell would also have to find a new place. It was messy but the best decision to make for us.

02 May, 2020

I want to see my marriage flourish. Full of joy and mischief. Laughter. Abundance. Deep union with each other. A strong and powerful couple, able to serve others in their quest for a better marriage. I want our marriage to be easy, like a Sunday stroll in the bush. Serene, happy, content.

I want Hunter to have a hunger for God. Lord, speak to his inner being, help him to dig deep to find his inner strength and worth in You.

I want our businesses to be a source of abundant blessings. That work will be fun and fulfilling. Hunter to apply for his builder's licence so he can expand his business. The travel agency to come through Covid19 stronger and blessed. Clients booking cheerfully and extravagantly.

I want to sell my home for a miraculous amount, that can only be seen as from Victory. That if my friend's home is the right home for us, then we will be able to purchase it for a good and right price. We will enjoy renovating it and turning the garden into a heavenly paradise. If You have somewhere even better for us, I pray that You would make our pathway clear, giving us both peace about it and excitement.

I want us as a couple to believe that we can and will buy many homes. Some to keep and own outright, some to sell, some to give away. Supernatural ability to buy when it does not seem possible, and divine knowledge on the right properties to buy. Victory's divine timing.

Our days became routine. I worked a couple of hours a day on refunds for my clients and then I would meet up with friends for a walk. We were under lockdown conditions and businesses were kept shut while the virus was bought under control. Hunter's work dried up, but he managed to secure a job disinfecting a work site. He hated it, but it was work. When he arrived home, we would go for a walk. I felt he found it easier to talk while we walked. I was under the belief that although things were not perfect, we were marching in the right direction and eventually we would sort through all our circumstances and Victory would win out. I was convinced that neither of us wanted a divorce as we did truly love each other and understood the covenant promise we both made in front of our family, friends, and God.

In July, Hunter and I moved over to my house to start six weeks of renovations. Harmony and Mitchell had bought us out of the apartment, so we had the funds to renovate my house and finish the renovations at our jointly owned home, which would enable us to purchase our new home. Harmony and Mitchell decided to move out as the renovations were going to be messy and loud. They found a delightful granny flat close by. Hunter worked on transforming my home by replacing the rotten verandahs, painting throughout the house, fixing all the doors and windows, literally transforming an okay house into a spectacular home. I was to clean, organise other trades, pick carpet and paint and pack everything up. I was excited and happy that I was about to sell my home so we could live together and reboot our marriage. Hunter worked long hours on the home and was very quiet. We discussed what needed to be done to have it all finished, but whenever I tried to talk about our new home he shut down and never engaged in the conversation. I just put it down to exhaustion, and silly me just thought once we had completed this mammoth job, we would be able to sit down and discuss our next move. I thought we were on the same page, but I started to get the sense that we most definitely were not. I realised we might not be able to afford the house we were interested in, but we needed to discuss this and other possibilities. I was willing to move to Hunter's suburb as my business was still closed, or even to move out of our city entirely. We could do that now as I had the opportunity to change the trajectory of my life, and my business could stay shut. I was just totally naive.

Chapter 20

THE BROKEN HEART

12 September, 2020

Yesterday, my house went on the market. Yesterday, my husband left me. Sinister has control. There is so much I want to say but I have no strength left in me. The pain is so intense. I never thought this would actually happen. I suppose I was just believing that Hunter would eventually want to fight for us, but unfortunately, he has no fight in him. He would prefer to give up and walk away. I realise he has only asked for a week apart, but who gets a week off marriage whenever they feel like it? Someone who does not live with you. Someone who does not have the guts to change, to search out what has gone wrong. I gave him the option of a 'friendship marriage', but now that I have had time to process things, I believe I have to let him go. I believe if we go down the friendship route he will just come back and take advantage of me just being friends, where nothing has to change. I believe that I have to accept that separation, whether temporary or permanent, is the best option. He is not going to change when he knows I will just keep loving him. I will not leave him; I will just keep living with him while he treats me terribly. I must let him go and pray he reaches out to God. He has to get desperate enough to search out God. He needs to search for the why. Why he stopped loving me, why he stopped loving God. Where did he become unstuck? No more band-aids. He needs to get on his knees.

In the meantime, I need to search myself. Turn to God, with my heart and tears and repent for the part I played in making this marriage collapse. Even though it might look like he is all to blame I know that somewhere within the past two years I did something that damaged him, and rather than coming to me with it, he buried it (like he has always done), until it became impossible for him to love me and to love himself. So, in this time of separation, I pray he searches out what triggered this and he learns to face it.

I have so much to sort through. No business, no home, no marriage. Wow, I have been here before, and I got through it. Victory never left me, He worked with me and held me close. I just was not expecting to have to do this twice in my life. I don't know that I can. I don't want to.

21 September, 2020 - email I sent to Hunter

I can't help myself; I have to write. It is just finding the right thing to write.

I know you are hurting because of the pain I am in. I believe God miraculously bought us together and we were so in love. I'm still so much in love with you but I need to set you free. This is the decision you have made, and I need to respect that. We are both broken people and I have stood on God's word in believing through our brokenness we can heal and have an amazing marriage, but I couldn't do it alone. We needed you to step up, to believe with us. Jesus and I, and I am sure yourself, are weeping over this. People leave their marriage because of abuse or adultery so I am not sure why we are. Why haven't we been able to have a breakthrough and seen restoration?

I have spent many hours praying and weeping and asking God for an answer. I believe our marriage is in the midst of a spiritual battle. Together we were going to make a difference in people's lives. Our children would see what a strong Christian marriage we had and emulate it. Now they get to see us broken and walking away from each other. It pains me to think how much we have let them down. I pray they forgive us for our selfishness.

Finally, as your wife I just want you to think about you. I believe that when you found out about the sale of your trophy heads you were devastated, and you did not share this pain with anyone. You retreated. I think this triggered your mind into protection mode and allowed depression to creep in. Since this event you have become withdrawn and cynical, life turned grey to you. It really hurt you and triggered all the emotional pain from your past. Ever since this moment you have been unable to talk, to believe in yourself and to stand up against Sinister's fiery darts. Sinister has used it as an opportunity to steal your joy and happiness. To distract you from where you were travelling, on a road full of possibilities. You may dismiss all that I am saying as hogwash, you may think what would I know, I've never really known you. Well, I've known the best of you. I fell in love with a man full of faith. A man with talent to turn derelict houses into palaces. That laughed with abandon at silly things. A generous and trustworthy man. Loving, caring and super sexy. A man who loves his children and will do anything to help people. Hunter, you are that man. Always believe that. Depression can steal all this from you, it can make you turn your back on us. It will make you retreat into yourself and live in denial. Please go see a professional, whether that is a doctor or a counsellor. Tell them you have lost the ability to communicate with those that love you. You are worth fighting for. You need to believe in yourself. I am praying that you don't just dismiss all that I am saying. I am your wife still and I am allowed to speak into and over your life.

I shall now set you free to do this journey of life alone, but I am here waiting and believing for your return.

I sold my beautiful home, five weeks after I placed it on the market. The price was lower than I wanted but it was fair. I was going to find it hard to say goodbye. This home was an absolute blessing and I loved living there. I never thought I would have been able to own a home again after losing my horse property. Victory had been good. It was now time for a new adventure. Who knew what lay ahead?

As for the travel agency, I was still in business, if you call refunding and maintaining bookings business. The borders were shut tight with no indication of when they might open. My landlords had been so gracious and allowed me to have six months' rent free, but they now wanted me to start paying again, which was fair enough. They offered half rent, which was very kind of them to do so. The government's support package was helping me keep the doors open. I realise I could close the office and work from home, but it wasn't just about the business, it was about community; without my office I wouldn't have my peeps. I needed the distraction of people, and I certainly would not get that at home by myself. I had two major decisions to make: where on earth was I going to live, and what would I do about my business?

The first task was finding a place to rent. I had no idea how awful this was going to be. I made a list and off I went. Some of these rentals I saw I would not even put a dog in. I was in shock that people actually lived like this, and real estate agents were showing us around. The houses that had potential, masses of people showed up for. I had no idea this was going to be so hard. After one inspection, I jumped back into my car and burst into tears. I had no idea what I was going to do. I sent Hunter a text telling him how dreadful this was and asking could he allow me from the goodness of his heart to move into the house that I half owned with him. It was a resounding "No", and if I tried to move in, I would lose all dignity. He did, however, agree to come see me so we could talk things out.

17 October, 2020 - email sent to Hunter

Thanks for coming over today. I know that was not easy for you, for both of us. I think it was well worth the discomfort. I thought I would put in writing what we talked about so you can process things. It is not easy remembering things when you are in a place of turmoil. I have no doubt I would have forgotten a lot of what we had said, but here goes. It was great talking through things with you and getting your input on the house, my rental options, my work and my father. It is a lot for me to decide on by myself. However, I think the best thing for me to do is try find myself a suitable rental and park myself there for a season. It eliminates you having to immediately get me off the mortgage and allows me to get a job and get some pay slips happening so I can get a mortgage if I decide to buy a unit.

Now let's talk about you. I can see how broken you are. You are making decisions that will cause you great pain and will wreak even more havoc in your life. I can only encourage you to turn to God. He will not let you down. As you spend more and more time with Him, He will reveal so many things and He will start to heal your hurts. He is a God you can fully trust. However, He has given you free will and you can continue to choose to make bad choices. He cannot stop you from doing that, but even when you do, He still loves you with such intensity. He is there in your dark places, hurting with you. Jesus knows what it feels like to be abandoned and alone while He hung on that cross. Not only does Jesus believe in you, but so do I. There is an old, kind, humble man in you. We believe in you and one day you will believe in yourself. There are hidden hurts inside your darkest corners that need to be exposed so that you can become fully redeemed, saved and alive.

Now time for us. I've said this before, and I will keep saying it. I will not walk away from you. I believe in us. You know how much you have hurt me and if I was a normal person, I would run a mile. But we both know I am not normal. I will keep praying for our marriage. It is worth saving. I am not expecting a five-minute fix. It is going to take a lot of time and determination, but the reward will be momentous. Tonight, had a sweet fragrance where two broken people could be vulnerable and honest without pressure. I will fight for us even if you don't have the strength to do so. Are you open to that, or are you still convinced that we will never be again? I believe tonight showed us both that with time and help and understanding we could repair what Sinister has been determined to destroy. Hunter, your walk with God is my first priority. Getting right with Him is more important than getting right with me.

Thank you once again for a sweet evening. Praying you get deep, restful sleep all week.

04 December, 2020

What a journey! Hunter sent me an email telling me I was very controlling, and I need to move on. It was a tough read. However, Victory has been speaking to me over the last couple of days, showing me, he wasn't wrong. Ouch! Hunter was hurting. I have been controlling, and probably out of fear. Fear that I was going to be divorced yet again. Fear of being alone. Fear of being broken. Then there is all my endless writing and lists which was just pride. Showing him how it should be. What is right and what is wrong?

I rang Hunter last night and apologised. What I was doing was wrong. I told him I was moving on. I wished him all the best. This is hard and it hurts so much but it is right. It is not my place to change him, it's God's. He might never change, that is not my problem. He is in God's hands. Let Him do a good work in him. I know he's gone; it is over. Such sorrow. We did have something amazing. Sinister took it out, but he does not win. Victory does. It might not look the way I want it to but it will be good and right.

Lord forgive me for my controlling prideful ways. Forgive me for striving to fix things. You are the fixer of all, forgive me for trying to take Your place. I humbly stand before you with my hands outstretched, fully surrendered. Your will be done. Thank you for doing such a good work in me. I do not know what tomorrow looks like, it is scary, but I know you have me. It will be full of joy and laughter. Most importantly it will be overwhelmed with Your love. I will walk each day with you. Take each moment in your embrace. All you, all me, all together. Thank you, Lord, for your redemptive healing.

12 December, 2020

Let me record the beautiful kiss from God that just happened. I have to find somewhere to live as Hunter is not going to allow me to move in with him, even as housemates. This is hard for me to accept, but I do not have a choice. So, I put it out there: I prayed that I wanted a granny flat or even a shack in the middle of a paddock surrounded by horses. Well guess what - that is exactly what God has given me. Through my community I was told about this place. Mrs Shacklady came to see me, and she liked me. I will be living in a cottage, literally in the horses' paddock. Plus, for every hour I work on the property, I receive $25 off my rent. Victory is in the detail. He loves me so much. I have a new home, a place to heal, a place to rest. He loves me so much and just wants me to know He is watching over me. This place is perfect, and exactly what I asked for.

I am still broken hearted and want my marriage

restored, so even though I have been blessed with the perfect home, I am sobbing because this is not the solution I was seeking. I feel unbelievably ungrateful and truly awful that I am not praising Victory for this total miracle. I _am_ truly grateful, and I can still continue to pray for my marriage. Praying is the best possible thing to do.

Even though I was attending the old church I went to before I met Hunter, I was really missing our church that we had been attending together. I had it in my head that it was his church, and therefore I would not be welcomed, plus it was an hour away from where I lived. I decided to make an appointment to see our pastors and have a chat. I am so grateful that I did. They said I was welcome to attend and not to worry about Hunter. He was also welcome. People might talk about us, but not for long, they would soon find something else to talk about. I felt relieved and very excited about staying where I felt I belonged. I soon joined the worship team as a backing vocalist. I was in my happy place. Singing in my church community. I would have never thought I would be singing again. Victory knew better.

Three days before Christmas I received court orders from Hunter regarding our financial settlement. This sent me into a tailspin. I could not believe he was sending me this just before Christmas, what a delightful present. He was asking for the costs of the renovations on my place plus full ownership of his home. I was shocked. We agreed to spend the money from the sale of the unit on our properties so we could buy one together, and at no time was I told that he was charging me for the work he had done, or that he was planning on leaving me. He knew he was going to walk out, but he never told me during the renovations that he was going to charge me for the work. It was our money that we used to do this, not his. I was a complete mess throughout the Christmas break. In total shock that this man I was in love with' was still demanding this from me, and believed he was absolutely entitled to it. Why was he wanting settlement? We had only been separated for three months - what about reconciliation? Sinister was having a Christmas field day. I was going to have to find myself a solicitor and fight for what I believed rightfully belonged to me. I hate divorce and so does Victory.

Chapter 21

SPIRITUAL JOURNEY

THE YEAR OF 2021 started with the financial settlement looming. I didn't want to deal with it, but I knew I had to respond as it was a legal document. I spent time praying for answers. I didn't want to declare war, but I most definitely didn't want Sinister to snatch what rightfully belonged to Victory. My nature wanted to give everything to Hunter, because I had the mistaken belief that if I did that, he would love me for it and return to me. I had to push that aside and make sure to look after me. What was fair and reasonable? How could we both come away from this, not happy, but at least content with the outcome? Add to this the total devastation I was feeling about my relationship and the now obvious conclusion that Hunter was definitely moving on. He did not want to fight for us; however, he did want to fight for money. This was where he was in life, ready to end us whilst I was still not willing to let go. I wanted complete reconciliation; I knew what we had was worth the fight. My emotions were topsy turvy, going round and round in my head all through the night. I had to make a decision, I had to make a stand on what I believed was right for me and pray that Hunter understood my decision. I was going to say no to his demands and make a counter offer.

I won't go into boring legal stuff, but eventually over three months, with a lot of tears from me, we agreed on a settlement. As my solicitor said, "if both of you are unhappy then it is a good result." For me it was not having the money or possessions, it was about the door of our marriage being shut. We'd had such grand plans to buy and flip homes, for Hunter to renovate and me to design. I had enrolled in an interior design course during Covid lockdown the previous year so I could enhance Hunter's business. I was still coming to terms with Sinister's destruction, and I was always looking for Victory to step up.

I had to try move forward, so I decided to change my studies from interior design to teacher's assistant. I loved designing homes but now it broke my heart every time I picked up a pencil to design. Teacher's assistant suited me as I have always loved teenagers. As well as this course I also decided to enrol in a course to enrich my spiritual journey. To learn more about the things of God and stretch my thinking capacity. It was going to be at least another year before travel would happen, so I had to keep myself busy and occupied. I do not like to stay stagnant. I did not want to be labelled lazy- which might stem back to the time when Ralph use to make me keep an account of my day. What I did know about myself is that I liked to have projects, and now I had two, as well as a small amount of Australian travel I was booking. I loved to learn, so I was excited about my courses. I did hear Victory whisper that I was also allowed to take a rest, to take a year off and learn to be still. I had never taken a chunk of time off, but this was the year for me to learn to be me and to enjoy my own company.

The first Saturday I tried this "doing nothing" thing, was tough. I had to convince myself to just sit outside and enjoy the things around me. I wanted to at least pick up a book and read, but Victory said no. Learn to be still, quiet the mind. It was hard, but I managed to do this for three hours. Now, several months later, I joyfully sit still and contemplate. During these quiet times, I have experienced the still, small voice of the Lord.

05 February, 2021

I am sitting outside my new home, the shack. I call it 'The Shack' because of the book of the same name. This shack in the book was a place where the Trinity helped the book's main character through his journey. As far as shacks go, mine is a very fancy one. I am watching the horses; it is a beautiful place to live. I am surrounded by my community. I should have nothing to complain about. My thoughts drift, of course to Hunter, and I know that I cannot keep living in the perpetual cycle of pain and then hope. I have to believe that God has a better plan and a better purpose for me. I need to live for today and be thankful for all God has given me. Victory is right here with me. Growing me, stretching my faith, encouraging me. Rejection is a hard pill to swallow, but I will not let it define me.

I laid all my pain down and *tried* to move on with my life I wish I could say that is exactly what I did. Not me, I could not walk away from Hunter. I believed in an 'us' so I decided in my head that if I could only have his friendship than that was enough. Who was I kidding? My heart was way too invested for just friendship.

15 April, 2021

Today Hunter is coming over. He came last Friday to help move my office and today he is coming over to put up the brochure racks. I had asked if he could buy the paint at trade cost for me and he offered to help. Last Friday was a great day together, we get along so well. It was so emotionally hard as I just cannot understand why he does not want to be with me. We work so well together. It is stupid. I can only think that it comes back to his walk with God. It is all too hard for him to humble himself and fight for what is right. I burst into tears when he drove away. I was drained. Well, I get to do it all again today. I get to plaster on a smile, encourage him and pretend I am happy. Tough gig. Victory, give me peace, strength, wisdom, and joy. Let Hunter know how much you and I love him. Open his heart. Protect mine. I pray that today's walls start to crumble. That he starts to believe that there is a better life for him, and she is standing right here.

Hunter started coming back to church. I was so happy to see him there, and people were welcoming him. We started meeting up after the service. We had some lovely chats and I often spoke to him about the idea of us moving to the country. My latest desire was to open a retreat and bed and breakfast. Somewhere people could come for restoration. A place of welcome, of tranquillity and joy. Find a place close to Sydney so I could keep a handful of clients and Hunter could come back to do any jobs that interested him. We would also be close to our grandchildren. I was praying that Victory would speak to Hunter's heart and give him the same desire. He had the skills needed to run a property and I had the hospitality skills to look after guests. Definitely a dream team. He wasn't opposed to the idea, but he would never commit to an 'us '. He could see the benefits of us being together, but not the means to get us back.

On June 1st I became a grandmother when Harmony and Mitchell had a healthy baby boy. It would not be until the end of the month when I would realise how important this moment would be. He was, and still is, an absolute blessing to us.

13 June, 2021

It has been nine months since Hunter walked away. It has been a tough nine months and it scares me that in three short months he can file for divorce. Oh, how I hate that word. It has been such a journey, so painful and yet so joyous. I have missed my husband so very much, but I have not regretted the hours I have spent in the presence of the Trinity (God, Jesus and the Holy Spirit). What I coin Victory. Sweet communion with almighty God, being able to pour out my heartache and pain, but also my dreams and visions. Nothing has gone unheard, all my tears, groans, cries, screams but also all my prayers, affirmations, declarations, praise and laughter. It has all been heard. There is great joy in the throne room of heaven. Battles are being fought and won; ground is being taken back. All that has been stolen is being restored. Victory has spoken. His will be done. There is still part of this season left but it is drawing to a close. New life, new buds are springing forth from the burnt-out trees and ashes. An abundance of life. Meadows of yellow sunflowers glorifying the magnificence of their creator. Scores of angels singing with a loud voice, "Holy, Holy is the Lord Almighty, for He has done great things." He has restored the ashes of my life into a cacophony of glorious wonder, of incredible colours, of amazing regrowth. All things restored, all things made new, new vision, new life. It is done. I declare this over my life.

My thoughts now jump, I was thinking how I could continue my life as is. Maybe buy an apartment, work part time at a local school and part time in my business. Be a Mooshka (grandmother). Sing on the worship team at church. I would not be unhappy. I would have fulfilment, I could be happy and content, but who am I kidding. It is just so predictable. So cliche. So boring. Not for me. Instead, I dream and have visions of "By the Grace, Retreat and B&B." A place of rest, of joy, and beauty. A place to be blessed, a sanctuary for the starving soul. Full of challenges, tough, hard work, exhausting mentally, emotionally, physically, and spiritually. Giving and speaking into people's lives. Being present to their pain, hurt and disillusionment. Caring for them, praying for them, speaking into their lives. Chaotic in its magnificence. Exhausting, but so rewarding. Victory bringing people to us so that we can pour out. I see it all so clearly, and I long for this next season. All in your timing, Victory.

I see it unfolding with the man God gave me. Not by myself, not with a friend or a business partner but with my fully restored husband. He catches my vision and understands it is our vision and he thrives. Such great joy and happiness, so many lives changed because of what Victory has done in us and through us. I just see it so clearly. Sitting on our verandah, sharing a wine (maybe even one we produced), talking about the miracles God has done. Laughing at the absolute absurdity of where we have come from, what we have been through and where we are walking, together with the Lord. Living in a home for anyone that needs rest to come stay.

Yes, I really do want the happily ever after.

At the end of June, due to a coronavirus outbreak, we went into lockdown. I was so disappointed as I had made plans for Hunter and I to go to the country together and have a look around. I was really looking forward to spending time with him and starting to make small steps towards repairing our marriage. I wanted us to have some fun together, away from our home environments so he could see what the revised version of us could look like. I was looking forward to getting out of Sydney and spying out the land I am hoping we could move to. I ponder why every time I think progress is happening, Sinister steps in and demolishes my plans. I can only think that it is because if Victory wins, we will be a strong force helping many others.

I was about to stare down four months of lockdown restrictions. Yet again I had to leave my office and work from home, sitting outside my shack watching horses whilst I worked. Not that there was much work to be done. I am so grateful that I have the drive to self-motivate. I could literally sit here and not see a soul, and dive into depression. Instead, I am using this time to study, write this book and make sure I ring people and check up on how they are doing. I was so blessed to have my grandson to distract me during these months. He kept us entertained and sane. This lockdown will have devastating consequences in years to come. People need people, and to not be able to socialise is not healthy. I have seen Hunter on a fairly regular basis during this time; because we are still married, we are allowed to see each other, even though we live in different local areas. We have been going on walks and had lots of talks. Our time together is always sweet. The only struggle I have is when I go to his place. He has robbed it of all joy. I have been eliminated from this home, the place we designed together. He has replaced bright lamps with dark green, almost black ones, he has taken anything of any colour away. The trophy heads are on display in the now renovated back room as well as a couple in the lounge. The only room with any colour is the mosaic bathroom. Don't get me wrong, the place is clean, neat, and tidy and very well presented but it lacks warmth. It is as if he has displayed his home perfectly, but it is lacking love. I do wonder if this is how he wants to present himself to the world, all neat and tidy- but inwardly, he is a broken-hearted man.

It was two days before we would have been separated for 12 months. Hunter would be able to file for divorce. I was desperately trying to stay positive. Over the past couple of months, I had been texting Hunter and asking if we could catch up. He would read my texts but take days to respond. I tried calling instead so I did not have to stress while waiting, but he did not answer my calls. I know what you are thinking. Why on earth did I keep persisting with a man that clearly had no respect for me? All I can say is, every time I told myself "Enough is enough," Victory would whisper in my ear, "do not quit, keep praying, do not let Sinister win."

Anyway, I had texted him and finally a couple of days before the official date he asked if he could come over and go for a walk. I agreed, of course, but I was thinking he was coming over to discuss divorce. We went for a lovely walk, talked about life but nothing about us, that was normally what would happen. He stayed for dinner but before he left, I asked about the divorce. I told him that the day had finally arrived, but I still did not want to end our marriage, that I still believed in us, and I wanted to do all I could to repair the damage. However, I could not stop him from filing, he had free will, and if that was what he wanted, then so be it. He was mostly silent, like he always is when trying to talk about the deep issues. He didn't know what he wanted. The issue is with Hunter, he was happy to just stay married, he did not plan on ever marrying again, so it was no big deal staying married to me. Whereas I wanted a marriage, not just an occasional walking buddy. I felt like he only spent time with me because during Covid lockdown he was not allowed to spend time with anyone else. I was his entertainment. But I needed him to make a decision. He did not comment, just hugged me goodbye and left.

Chapter 22

A PLAN AND A PURPOSE

IT HAS BEEN 18 months since Hunter walked away. I still cry every day, but I so wish I didn't. I'd love to tell you I am fully restored and bouncing with joy, that Victory has reigned supreme. I can't tell you that. My days are still a struggle. I still miss him terribly; I still have such a huge desire to be married. I do not choose to be single; I married this man because I loved him with all my heart and wanted to spend forever with him. I don't understand what went wrong, how do you recover from such trauma when you cannot work through what happened. What did I say, what did I do to push him so far away that he never desired to walk back? I see and read about relationships constantly and most people at least try to reconcile, they fight for their marriage, it might not happen but at least they tried. Hunter, though, just shut the door of his heart and refused to open it even an inch. "I do not want you, just leave me alone."

I don't want you thinking that all I do is sit around all day every day on my shack patio lamenting the demise of my marriage. I do sit with my thoughts and process them, and ask the Lord why, and He always listens and cares. But he also strengthens me to get up and get moving, so I do. I make sure I spend lots of time with family and friends. If I can't see them, I ring them. I now work part time at a high school in the learning support department, and it is good for me to be around lots of people. It is a challenge for me to work for someone, to have to be accountable to my head of department - the last time I had a boss I was 23! I can't just make my own decisions, there is a process to be followed. I've had to be pulled into line and told I couldn't do things my way. I didn't take this well, and thought "how dare they criticise me", but they know what they are doing, I don't. I had to understand that it wasn't criticism, it was explaining what is expected of me. I try to make sure that somewhere during my school day I encourage someone, whether that be a student or a teacher. We all need to be loved. The job isn't hard, but it is a challenge for me, I know the travel industry and I excel in it, but this school thing is a whole different ballgame.

I still have my travel business - I go to the office straight after school. The industry is finally picking up, people are wanting to travel, mainly to go see family overseas, while the holiday business is still a little slow. My days are busy, usually starting at 6am cleaning out horse stables, then off to work at the school and my office, before going home and putting the horses to bed. It is good to be busy. When I stop for the day, and I have to make a meal for one, this is when I find it tough. I should be cooking dinner for my husband and I. Best solution to this time of day is to crank up the music. I never put on the news, that will never make anyone happy! Music is my go-to.

The biggest joy of this year is that I am now a worship leader at my church. I never thought I would ever have the opportunity to worship lead. I did not feel my voice was good enough, or that I had the confidence or courage to stand and lead the congregation. I might feel insecure, but God has put the boldness of a lioness inside of me. I have been pushed down, put in boxes of inadequacy my entire life, but God has placed a fighting spirit within me. He has and will continue to pull apart the boxes that I have been shoved into, and he will fill me with his strength to not only carry on, but to also worship lead others into the throne room of heaven. It is an honour and a privilege to stand before my church family and lead them. I am forever grateful that the leader of our music team encouraged me to step out in faith and lead. My church is allowing people to serve who may not be professional or incredible in their gifts, but who have a humble heart and are willing to be vulnerable so others can see and experience what God is doing in our lives.

My life is full. It might not be what I had planned but Victory always has a way forward. Sinister wants nothing more than to shut me down, keep me boxed up or in a puddle on the floor but he does not win, God does.

I truly wanted to believe Hunter would return, that he would eventually want to reconcile. I had all the promises, visions, and scriptures, so of course he would! I had to understand that he wasn't going to. The Lord had to graciously show this to me, I had to see it to believe it, otherwise I would keep holding onto hope and keep believing for his return. Hunter's intentions were revealed when one of my closest friends rang to say she'd just got 'matched' to him on a dating site. My poor friend felt terrible as she knew how much I was praying for reconciliation. Hunter had listed on his profile that he was single, he wanted to meet someone who was 'drama-free', wanted to go away for weekends and loved to banter. I could not believe that he was back on the site where we met, and he was saying he was single. This is exactly what he did to me. When we met online, he said he was single, yet he was still married. Once he believed our relationship was going somewhere, that was when he started the divorce process. I would not have initiated the conversation with him on a dating site if I had been aware of his marital status at the time. Maybe once I had learnt about it, I should have run a mile but by then I was in love and fully convinced that it was just an oversight of his, and being a male just had not gotten around to doing it. My thoughts today are very different. He has a wife who truly wants to reconcile but he wants another woman to satisfy his needs.

My daughter was incensed that he would go back to online dating whilst still married. She sent him a text message stating her grievances. His response was to say that it wasn't all his fault, that he was sorry for the pain he had caused, but that we weren't the only ones hurting. He was also upset that I was still attending our church, because it meant that he felt he could no longer attend.

This was the only communication from him in four months. I finally have an idea of where we are at. Here I was thinking giving him time and space was letting him evaluate our marriage and this would lead to him eventually returning. But in fact, he was making sure by leaving me alone I would understand he was through with us.

Despite his bitterness about me continuing in our church, I won't stop going there. I have made many beautiful friends and this church family has embraced me and loved me through a very difficult season. Hunter stopped coming a long time ago now. I'm sad that he made this choice.

I understand that not everything was his fault, but I really do wish he could have told me what I had done wrong. I was, and still am willing to do anything to repair the damage I have done. I suppose the difference between him and me is I am going to see a counsellor regularly. I am willing to do what it takes, I am open to change, and I truly love him. He does not want to do anything except walk away. His heart and mine are complete opposites.

The day came when we had to file for divorce. I never wanted to do this, I only wanted reconciliation, but with Hunter only stonewalling and leaving me hanging, I was left with no choice. The day I went around to collect our marriage certificate so I could proceed, I saw through the front window a woman's clothing and bra on the floor of the bedroom. I had been replaced. They were both there in the lounge room when I knocked, and she was sitting in my chair.

Shame and guilt were written all over his face. I had no intention of causing a scene. I cannot believe I went back and faced that nightmare, and I stood my ground. I needed that certificate so I could file, and he would no longer be lying to his dates. It was hard, but I did it, and I was grateful for my friends who were waiting for me afterwards to have a long lunch, a cry and a debrief.

It is hard being forced to do something that should not have to be done but it is clear that he has moved on. It is now time for me to do the same. I will still cry, and that is ok, but I will survive. I will become stronger, and I will go on to help others who are lost in the wilderness of unbelief and grief. I often contemplate on just how many women (I know there are men too, but I am a woman) have been thrown out with the trash. We have such a deep desire to be loved and to love but it is so often not fulfilled. Men walk away and start the cycle again with another. The world is full of broken and damaged women but given time these women will grow strong, and they will be full of joy again. We might not get another opportunity to love again within a marriage, but we will get given countless opportunities to love others. We will also go deeper in communion with God, we will learn to hear his voice with a pure intimacy that can only be found in the stillness, in the quiet place.

I understand that the courage to surrender comes from knowing that love and pain can hurt us, and try to take us out, but that we can stand firm in God's love, knowing he has us in the palm of his hand. I will see the Victory.

Epilogue

M y JOURNEY IS not yet over. We were never promised a life of ease, this is definitely no walk in the park for me. I have always had to fight for what I want. It is more than just life; it is a spiritual battle. There are angels and demons waging war and we must stand strong in our belief that Victory wins.

Hunter told me my life was full of drama, but I refuse to accept this. My life is full of adventure, it is never boring. I live and love with my all. I am a deeply feeling person in a messy world. When I stand before God in heaven, I will be able to say, "Well God, earth was one huge adventure for me, I am looking forward to heaven being one gigantic adventure."

Reflections of 2021

As I sit here looking at dark clouds interspersed with highlights of sun, the storm has passed, the victory is won. Love shines brightly down upon the weary soul.

The battles I have fought, the relentless journey of pain I have been walking is behind, but also still in front of me. It is a long journey, a process that takes the time it takes. I relish in the things that have been accomplished. Delight in all that the Lord has revealed. The endless supply of love, kisses, revelations, and hugs. The tough days, the good days, the lonely days, the busy days, the days of solitude and comfort. Many hours hanging out with God, looking always outward, over the paddocks, into the sky, moaning and groaning yet growing and learning. The gift of time, of courage, of learning and standing strong. These are precious jewels from above. The relentlessness of not letting go, of believing in the midst of total disbelief, holding onto the promises bestowed upon me, knowing my God hears my cries of prayers. Teaching me to open up myself, to be more vulnerable than ever before and in total vulnerability God pours a reservoir of love, pure crystal-clear love, flowing down from heaven above, out of the throne room of heaven.

The journey of discovery, of finding out who I am, that I am Lila, a daughter of the most high. I am precious in his sight, I am called, I am a worship warrior, I am God's beloved. He is happy with me and so am I.

I have filed for divorce; it was not easy for me to do but it was important for me to stand strong in who I am and boldly close the door. I still believe in miracles, the happily ever after, and so I cannot help but secretly hold out hope that he will one day soon reconcile with me. I could still see us together, building a retreat and a B&B, building a life together.

It is not unheard of; divorced couples do return to each other at times. However, Hunter has free will and what I do not doubt is that even if I never see him again, I will still have the Victory.

It is heartbreaking to see the end of my second marriage, but Victory has a plan, and dare I say a better plan. Life is a journey we must embrace no matter the hardship and battle because God wants to pour out his favour, grace, and mercy. He wants us to live life to the full in complete Victory, no matter the cost at the time to us. We cannot see our entire span of time, but God can. He knows what he is doing, we just cannot see what is being done in the secret place.

I did not write this story to disparage the men in my life. I do not understand why I have been treated the way I have. I have learnt over the past years that abuse takes on many forms. It does not have to be physical abuse. I am not saying my marriages were abusive, but my husbands definitely neglected me. They neglected to take care of me, to communicate with me, to fight for me and to stay committed to me. I suppose these are forms of abuse and I have had to accept that at times I've attracted that. I have had to learn to believe in me, to know that I am worthy to be loved, that it is okay to be the person I am. I am a storyteller, I talk too much, I cannot keep a secret, I have high expectations, I like beautiful things, new cars, and fancy holidays. I love to laugh and be silly. I love colour and joy and to sing. I love with abandon and do not give up easily the things I believe in. Hunter wanted a sedate life, without complication, affordable, a life of predictability, a life heading towards a comfortable retirement. He grounded me, kept me from taking too bold a step, while I made him think bigger with more possibilities. We truly did complement each other.

If you are in a place in your relationship where you suspect a form of abuse, please do not ignore it. You are worthy so please seek help. Start with your Heavenly Father who will never abandon you.

I have written this to let you know that although life is hard - and I have cried buckets of tears - God collects our tears – and I am sure He has an ocean full of mine. My story is not spectacular, there is no divine healing, or being stranded in a desert and rescued. My story is an ordinary life. In this life I have learnt even the best plans often have to be laid down. If I had seen what was in front of me before I was even born, would I have wanted to do this journey called life? My answer of course is yes. The journey is hard but the many miracles and breakthroughs along the way are extraordinary. There is a God in heaven who does see our pain. He is not a magician who is just there to wave his magic wand and see us all walk the easy road. He wants us to learn, to experience and most importantly put all our trust in Him. I will never turn my back on my Lord and Saviour. Without the Trinity I could not have survived this journey. God has held me close, built me up, helped me and promised me that no matter what it looks like now, Victory is mine. I have pulled on my pink boots, and I boldly jump into all the black puddles set before me. They are only puddles, and with the right pink boots on I can walk right through them. My task is to keep praying, keep believing, keep holding on. Live the life I have been given to the fullest. But most importantly above all else, to love the Lord my God with all my heart and to love others as I love myself.

Acknowledgments

I want to thank my daughters for being exceptional children, yes, we had our moments, but the two of you made being a parent easy. God blessed me with supportive, kind, and intelligent girls who I can always count on to meet me on the other side of my puddles. Their support and love are truly valued. Plus, they married great men, I must have taught them something.

I want to thank my parents, despite my story indicating they were unaware of what was happening in my life I knew they were there for me; I just didn't know how to share my pain with them. They have always loved me and lifted me up in prayer throughout my life. They are incredible grandparents and went above and beyond to help me parent my daughters. When my life fell apart, they stood by me, dad and his humour always looking for the rainbow after the rain.

My journey is made sweeter by my many friends, thank you for helping me laugh through the moments and encourage me to keep looking forward. You know who you are.

Special thanks to my editor, Clare Bruce also Cassandra from The Digi Dame for my awesome book cover design and all my lovely extras, and Miriam for proofreading, you all helped make my book shine.

I do not want to be the typical cliche girl because I have always liked being different but here it needs to be said, thank you God, Jesus, and the Holy Spirit for never leaving me, always loving me unconditionally and teaching me to always look to my future because it will be epic. God, I love being your daughter.

My readers, thank you for taking the time to read about my journey. We all have a story to tell, it is growing and learning whilst on the journey that counts. Never lose hope, never quit, you never know what will happen next. Live in the adventure.

If you have read this book and just need someone to share your journey with, please contact me via email ~ lila@pinkbootspublishing.com or my website pinkbootspublishing.com I would love to hear from you.